JESSICA BECK

THE DONUT MYSTERIES, BOOK 34

SCARY SWEETS

Donut Mystery #34 Scary Sweets
Copyright © 2017 by Jessica Beck All rights reserved.
First Edition: September 2017

No part of this book may be reproduced, scanned, or distributed in any printed or electronic form without permission. Please do not participate in or encourage piracy of copyrighted materials in violation of the author's rights. This is a work of fiction. Names, characters, places, and incidents either are the product of the author's imagination or are used fictitiously, and any resemblance to actual persons, living or dead, business establishments, events, or locales is entirely coincidental.

Recipes included in this book are to be recreated at the reader's own risk. The author is not responsible for any damage, medical or otherwise, created as a result of reproducing these recipes. It is the responsibility of the reader to ensure that none of the ingredients are detrimental to their health, and the author will not be held liable in any way for any problems that might arise from following the included recipes.

The First Time Ever Published!

The 34th Donut Mystery.

Jessica Beck is the *New York Times* Bestselling Author of the Donut Mysteries, the Classic Diner Mysteries, the Ghost Cat Cozy Mysteries, and the Cast Iron Cooking Mysteries.

For P, home is indeed where the heart is!

It's Fright Week in April Springs, a time filled with special events leading up to Halloween, but the celebration is in jeopardy when a body is found in the middle of the night on the platform of the dunking booth under the town clock. Suzanne and her mother decide to investigate, and soon secrets from the past resurface and threaten the present in a very real way.

CHAPTER 1

WHEN I LOOKED OUT INTO the darkness from my
donut shop front window, I saw a face leering in at
me from the other side of the glass.

I'm not usually prone to screaming, but I'm not ashamed to
admit that I lost it when I saw a set of bloodshot eyes staring
right back at me.

It had been time for my morning break, if you could call four-
thirty a.m. "morning," and since I was working alone, I wasn't
going to have any company. Emma Blake, my assistant at Donut
Hearts and a good friend as well, was no doubt home asleep,
where most folks with any sense probably were at the moment.

Not me. I was up making donuts for the citizens of April
Springs, North Carolina, just like I did five days a week. On
those glorious two days out of seven that I wasn't working,
Emma and her mother, Sharon, took the reins of Donut Hearts,
not that I was known for sleeping in, even though I could have.
My husband, retired state police inspector Jake Bishop, was a
morning person as well, but I still beat him up by at least two
hours every morning I wasn't working. While he slept, I usually
worked a crossword puzzle, read one of the cozy mysteries I
loved so much, or spent my time daydreaming about new donut
treats I could make.

It took me a second to realize that I wasn't looking at a person on the other side of the window after all. It was simply a Halloween fright mask, though why anyone would choose to buy one, let alone try to scare me to death with it, was beyond me. I cautiously opened the front door and saw that someone had popped the mask onto an old broom handle, and then they'd leaned it against the glass in such a way that I was sure to see it when I came back out into the dining area of the shop. If that had been their goal, they had succeeded beyond their wildest expectations. What troubled me most about the mask's presence was that I knew it hadn't been there when I'd come in a short hour and a half earlier. I might not be the most observant person in the world when I first wake up, but *that* I'm sure that I would have noticed.

I tried to look around, but I couldn't see much of anything at all until I stepped outside into the cool night air. It was October, and I knew that before long, the light jacket I'd grabbed on my way out of the shop would no longer be heavy enough to battle the chilly air. Once I was out in the darkness after I'd carefully locked the front door behind me, I could see that the Boxcar Grill sported a single porch light that provided barely any illumination at all. Directly across the street, Paige Hill's bookstore had a pair of small candlestick lights in the front window that served to highlight all of the spooky titles she'd chosen for the week of scary festivities. As I took a step farther out onto Springs Drive, a safe enough thing to do at that time of night since there was rarely any traffic, I realized that the spotlight pointed to the dunking booth was lit up.

That hadn't been on when I'd come in earlier, either. Odd. I decided to investigate, but not before double-checking to be sure that I'd locked the front door behind me. It paid to be careful, especially when I was all alone.

Walking down the street toward the lights, I started to wish that I'd brought the baseball bat I kept under the cash register for protection with me. It would feel good in my hands at the moment, but I wasn't going back for it. As I approached City Hall and then neared the Town Clock where the booth had been set up, I could hear carnival music playing softly in the distance.

Evidently I wasn't the only one out at that time of day.

The booth, a brightly colored display piece featuring a glass front panel, had been spooked up a little from its normal carnival appearance, with tiny rubber bats hanging from it, loads and loads of fake spider webs strewn all about, and dark-blue lights that gave everything around it an eerie shadow.

Had some bored teenager flicked the ON switch that generated the music and the lights after leaving me a nasty little surprise at my window? I started looking for a way to turn the entire display off when I saw that the booth's bench seat, rigged to collapse the moment the center target had been struck by a softball, wasn't empty.

A hefty man dressed in a suit was sitting there, wearing a pumpkin mask that the folks who allowed themselves to be dunked for charity wore.

"Excuse me," I said, my voice quivering a little as I said it. The reason for the tremor in my voice wasn't just because it was the last week in October in our little section of the mountains of North Carolina. "Are you okay?"

There was no answer.

"Hello? Sir?" I asked again, being a little more insistent this time.

Again, there was no response.

The way I saw it, I had three choices. I could climb up the ladder myself and check on the masked man from behind, I could hit the target and send him plunging into the water where he'd be easier to identify and retrieve, or I could call the police.

3

I knew that I had a reputation in town for doing some foolhardy things, but I opted to call the police instead of taking direct action myself. Besides, it was an easy decision to make, since the station was less than ten yards away from where I stood.

Officer Dan Bradley, a relatively new policeman on the force, answered at once. "April Springs PD, Bradley speaking."

"Officer Bradley, this is Suzanne Hart. Somebody's perched on the dunking-booth bench, and I'm not at all sure if he's still alive."

He snorted once before he replied. "Ms. Hart, I'm getting tired of this foolishness, and it's only just started. I can't believe we have another six days of this. Whose idea was it to have a Halloween Fright Week, anyway?"

"The mayor's girlfriend suggested it, but I don't really want to talk about that right now. What are you going to do about the body?"

"Ten bucks says that it's just another dummy rigged up to look like a person, but I'll be right there to see for myself." Almost as an afterthought, he added, "Just in case, don't touch anything."

"I'm not climbing up on that ladder, and as far as I can tell, it's the only way I can get to him, so you don't have to worry about that," I said.

After I hung up, I found myself really wishing that I'd something to defend myself with. I felt vulnerable standing there in the darkness. The policeman might have thought it was just something rigged up to look like a dead body, but I knew better. We were dealing with something far more serious than a dummy.

Less than a minute later, Officer Bradley showed up, looking peeved as he rubbed his hands together. "It's gotten colder."

"It usually does this time of year," I said as I pointed to the body. It certainly didn't look like a stuffed dummy to me, but then again, I didn't have an expert's eye for that type of thing, regardless of what some folks in town might have thought. Lately I seemed to be a magnet for murder, as much as I wished that it weren't true.

Officer Bradley climbed the steps of the dunking booth, but as he got to the top and was in a position where he was finally close enough to the body to see it in detail, he stiffened a little. "It's the real thing," he said as he reached forward and pulled the body toward him. His position on the ladder was precarious at best, and he and his charge both nearly tumbled into what had to be freezing water, but he managed to correct himself, and a minute later, he had him safely on the ground.

"Who is it?" I asked as I leaned over the officer's shoulder for a better look. Whoever it had been was clearly dead, but I was surprised about something.

I didn't recognize him.

On closer examination, I saw in the eerie blue light that his suit was threadbare at the pant cuffs, and his tie was clearly faded. His hair was in need of a trim, and there was evidence on his chin that he'd botched shaving, or else he'd used a dull razor. To top it all off, he had a bit of a moon-shaped face that somehow fit with the mask I'd found on him when I'd first seen him.

"Do *you* recognize him?" I asked Officer Bradley.

"No, but then again, I don't know everyone in April Springs."

"Well, I just about do, and he's a stranger to me. What do you suppose killed him?"

As I leaned forward to see if I could get a better look at the body, the police officer put a restraining hand on my shoulder. "Ms. Hart, maybe you should head back to the donut shop. I need to call the chief and see how he wants to handle this."

"He really is dead, isn't he?" I asked, ignoring the request.

"I can't find a pulse," the officer said a little more abruptly. "Let me do my job, okay?"

"Fine. I'll be at the donut shop if you need me," I said.

"I'm sure Chief Grant will be along later," the officer replied.

"If he does, he knows where to find me," I said.

As I started back down the street, I thought about the mask leaning on my window, and I wondered if it could possibly be related to the murder. I turned back to tell Officer Bradley about it, but he was already on his radio, summoning his boss, no doubt.

I'd mention it to the chief when I saw him, but in the meantime, the police officer was right.

I had donuts to make. The timer in my pocket went off as I approached the front door of the shop, and as I went back inside, I decided to take Smiling Jack back in with me. That was the nickname I'd just given him. Making it funny and trite somehow took the sting out of the way I'd found him staring at me earlier.

As I dove back into the dough for the raised donuts, I couldn't help wondering who I'd seen and how he'd died. I doubted that it had been natural causes, though I hadn't seen any wounds or telltale blood on him. It was hard to guess how he'd managed to get himself up onto that dunking bench in the middle of the night, one of the oddest places to die I'd ever seen, but at least it wasn't my job to figure it all out.

As I worked to create the yeast donuts to complement the cake ones I'd made earlier, I couldn't help wondering if the dead man would be the end of the Fright Week festivities before they had even had a chance to begin. The entire concept had been the mayor's new girlfriend's idea, and Cassandra Lane had turned out to be a force to be reckoned with. She'd come up for an extended visit from Charlotte after George had unsuccessfully tried living there first and, surprising all of us, not the least of all our dear mayor, she'd taken to small-town life as though she'd been born to it.

As I worked with the yeast dough, I lost myself in the process, doing my best to forget about the sight of the man's dead body as I cut out the rounds and holes and allowed them to rest before dropping them into the boiling oil in rapid order.

As I finished up the last of them, I was surprised to hear the front door open. Had I forgotten to lock it behind me? Only two other keys existed, at least that I was aware of. Jake had one, and Emma had the other, and I wasn't expecting either one of them.

Grabbing a roll cutter, I peeked through the kitchen door to see who was visiting Donut Hearts before I was officially open for business.

"What are you doing here on your day off?" I asked my assistant as I eased my roller down from its attack position.

Emma looked at me sheepishly as she explained, "I couldn't sleep, and I had a great idea we could try before you open the shop for the day."

"You're getting as bad as me. You know that, don't you?" I asked her with a grin. "This place has a way of consuming your life."

"Hey, I have a life," she protested feebly. "Besides working here, I go to school, and I also have a boyfriend. Don't forget that."

"How is Barton doing?" I asked. Emma was dating a culinary miracle worker who had aspirations of opening his own restaurant someday. In the meantime, he was providing delicious fare at the hospital cafeteria, much to everyone's delight.

"He's itching to get started on opening a location of his own," she said. "Now that Emily is back at Two Cows and a Moose, he was wondering if you might allow him to make that space into a restaurant."

My dad had left me a building along Viewmont Avenue. It had been a lawyer's office at one point, Jake had taken a turn there with an aborted attempt to be a private investigator, and it had even served as an emergency location for my friend's newsstand while she'd had her place renovated due to a broken water pipe, but I wasn't at all sure about having it be a restaurant, no matter how good the cause might be. "I'll have to think about that," I said as diplomatically as I could muster, trying to think of some way to decline her request graciously.

When I looked at Emma, I saw that she was grinning at me. "I was just teasing, Suzanne. It wouldn't work at all."

"I'm relieved you know that," I said.

After Emma shrugged, she said, "Your name did come up in our conversation last night, but I told him that he was crazy."

"He really wanted to use that building for his restaurant?" I asked her, surprised that Barton would even consider it.

"No. He wants Donut Hearts."

"What? But he can't have it. It's mine," I said.

Emma nodded as she explained, "During the morning, sure, but his idea was that this place is empty from the time for lunch all the way to the dinner hour. He thinks it's a perfect solution to use this space when it's empty. Don't worry. I told him that he was crazy."

I started to agree with her when I thought about it for a moment. Was it really that bad an idea? "Am I wrong, or does that make sense in a way?" I asked her. Once I got over the shock of sharing my space, I knew that it could work. I hardly ever used the building after eleven in the morning, so why shouldn't Barton get some use out of it, too?

"Suzanne, it's crazy," she said. "Isn't it?" she added after a moment's pause, sounding unsure of herself now.

"Tell you what. Let me think about it first, okay? Don't say anything to Barton about it quite yet."

"There's no worry about that. I'm still not sure it's a very good idea," she said.

"Speaking of good ideas," I said, "what did you have in mind earlier?"

"About what?" Had she already forgotten about why she was there?

"I presume you didn't get up, get dressed, and come over here in the dark just to ask me about Barton using my office building for a restaurant," I said.

"No, I have what I think might just be a great idea," she said. "Come back into the kitchen and I'll show you."

I followed her into the workspace, and as I iced the donut holes still waiting for their sweet drenching, Emma moved to the supply closet and gathered a few things together as though she owned the place. I suppose that two days a week she did. I'd had a little trouble at first sharing my space with her. How would it feel to have Barton working there, too? I wasn't sure if I could bring myself to do it, but I was a big fan of the man, and if I could help him out, maybe I should.

Emma grabbed some confectioner's sugar, some vanilla extract, a cup of water, and a few piping bags and tips. Her last stop was for food coloring, and I wondered what she was up to. It didn't take long to find out. After Emma mixed up a sizable batch of icing, she divided it into five small bowls. To four of these she added drops of orange, black, red, and blue, leaving the last bowl white.

The tinted icings were all quite vivid, but she grabbed the white first. After grabbing a small round donut hole, Emma made a perfect little white circle on one side of it. Setting that piping bag aside, she grabbed another and filled it with the blue icing. Within the white circle, she made a smaller blue one, and by the time she was ready for the black icing, I had it ready and handed it to her. It hadn't been all that difficult following her line of thought. One perfect black dot, the smallest of all, went into the center of the icing, and she held it up for me to see when she had finished.

It was a perfect confectionary eyeball.

"We can do green and brown, too," she said, "and we can sell them for Fright Week."

"I love it," I said as I started laying out more donut holes, ready for the same doctoring. "Shall we do them all?"

"We'd better leave a few plain for the traditionalists," Emma said with a grin. "Not everyone might like to eat an eyeball, no matter how tasty it might be."

"I suppose. What about the orange and red icings?"

"I thought the white icing could be fangs on some of the donuts, and red could be blood tipping them," she said. "Or is that too gruesome?"

"I don't know. Let's make one and see," I said. Fright Week might not run to its culmination, but if it did, I was going to do my best to get into the spirit of things. It was unfortunate that a man had died in such a public place during the beginning of the festival, but it very well could have been from natural causes. At least I hoped that was what it was. In the meantime, it felt good to get my mind off of finding the body earlier, no matter how gruesome the current task might seem to a casual observer.

We had great fun decorating donuts in all kinds of different ways, and by the time I was ready to open, our front display looked quite a bit different than I'd originally planned. Gone were the plain donut holes, and in their places were dozens of eyes peering out in sweet splendor. What had once been plain cake donuts had now been transformed into orange and black cats, bats, and cauldrons bubbling over with white icing. There were white icing cobwebs everywhere, and a few filled donuts had been covered with black icing, with only two white dots signifying eyes for those as well. We had to make more tinted icing in the end, but I didn't mind.

The only thing left was to stand back and see how folks reacted to what we'd done. As six a.m. approached, opening time for Donut Hearts, Emma said, "That was so much fun, you shouldn't even pay me for my time."

"Of course you're getting paid. You've been on the clock since you showed up," I said. "Care to make a few more dollars, since you're already here?" I asked her lightly.

"I might. What did you have in mind?"

"You can either help me sell our treats up front, or you can do the dishes," I said with a grin.

"Any chance I can do a little of both?" she asked. "I'll do dishes before the kids start showing up, and then I'll work out here with you a bit so I can see their reactions."

"That sounds like a plan to me," I said. "Thanks for coming in, Emma. Do you have any more ideas?"

"You'd better believe it," she said. "How about holding a decorating contest?"

"We've had those before. Sure, why not?" I asked. I'd been hoping for something a little more over the top from her.

"The thing is, it's not just for kids this time," she said with a grin. "We can have different age divisions, just like they do in races. Sure, the kids can enter their own heats, but so can the grownups. Can you imagine the seniors division? It could be a blast."

"Max could coordinate it with his group of actors," I said. My ex-husband, Max, also known as the Great Imposter, was an actor who loved directing stage plays using seniors at the center when he wasn't working. His twist was that he used productions that sported youth-based themes, which were always a hit with the community. Seeing geriatric Romeos and Juliets was a real hoot, especially when they were played straight, which they always were.

"We could do one division per day, leading up to Halloween," Emma said. "I'll get started on the posters. What should the prizes be? I know money's kind of tight right now, so it needs to be something else."

"Money's always tight," I said with a smile. "But I've got something better than that."

"What did you have in mind?"

"We feature the winner of each division, along with their photograph, in the window, and besides that, they get a free donut a week for all of November. To top it off, the grand prize winner gets a donut a week for the entire year. How's that for incentive?"

"I love it," she said.

"Then get started on it and set your PR machine loose on it," I said as I rearranged a few eyeballs before we opened.

"You know that Dad will be happy to advertise it for free," Emma said. I'd forgotten all about her father for a moment. Ray Blake owned the town's only local newspaper, and it staggered the imagination when I wondered how he'd cover my earlier discovery.

One thing was sure.

It would be sensationalized beyond recognition, if Ray had anything to say about it.

After Emma disappeared in back, I was almost ready to open the shop for the day when I heard a tap on the front door.

Chief Grant had finally made his way down to my shop, and just in time, too.

It appeared that the two of us were going to have a little chat about what, or more importantly who, I'd found earlier and what it might mean to Fright Week and our sleepy little town.

CHAPTER 2

"WHAT HAPPENED TO HIM?" I asked before the chief could even say a word.

"I'm still not sure," Chief Grant said as he took a seat at the counter. "Is the coffee fresh, by any chance?"

"Coming right up," I said. "Would you like a donut to go with that?"

"I'd better not," the chief said as he patted his stomach. "I'm learning that this job has a tendency to add the pounds, you know? Sitting behind a desk makes it tough for me to get much exercise."

"I can imagine," I said. "I'm on my feet all day, so at least I don't have that problem."

After the chief had taken a few sips of coffee, he said, "Excellent. That's better. Thanks."

"So, what happened to that man? Did he die of natural causes, or did someone murder him?"

"I don't have a clue," he said with a sigh.

"Seriously?" I'd known the chief since he'd first joined the force, and I didn't think I'd ever seen him so stymied by something.

"Suzanne, I'm not a doctor or a coroner. I'm just a cop. If there are obvious signs of trauma, I'm pretty good at being able to tell how someone died, but I'm going to have to leave this one to the experts. It could have been natural causes, or it might just have been something else."

"That covers just about the entire spectrum, doesn't it?" I asked as Emma started to poke her head out of the kitchen. When she saw the police chief sitting at the counter, she quickly ducked back inside, though I knew I'd be getting questions from her later.

"I suppose it does." He glanced at the display racks, looked away for a second, and then he looked back at them. "Are those eyeballs?"

"That's what we were going for. Why? Do you like them?"

He grinned at me. "Yeah, those are pretty sweet. Give me a blue one, would you?"

I served him the donut hole he'd requested, and he ate it with relish, but only after admiring it a little longer close up. "Those are really clever."

"I don't deserve the credit. It was all Emma's idea," I said.

"I'm sure you had a hand in it, too."

"Chief, is Fright Week going to be cancelled?" I asked him as I topped off his coffee.

"Apparently not," the chief said with a frown. "I tried to get the mayor to shut the entire thing down just in case this turns out to be homicide, but he wouldn't hear of it. If it was murder, it's going to be a nightmare with all of the visitors slated to come. The truth is, since Cassandra came to town, he's not as measured as he used to be."

That was true enough, at least in my opinion, but I didn't think it was always necessarily a bad thing. Cassandra had somehow managed to get our grumpy mayor to loosen up and smile every now and then, and as far as I was concerned, that was all right with me. "Does that mean that you're not treating the dunking booth like a crime scene? Is that what you're saying?"

"I'm doing everything in my power to secure things, just in case. We drained the water, we took samples to be analyzed, and I even had someone check the wiring on the lights in case he was electrocuted. I did a quick search of his body. The man was as hairy as a bear, and if there was any evidence on his body, I couldn't find it. There was no sign of blunt force trauma, or any other cause of death as far as I could see. I've impounded the dunking booth just in case, and the company that provided it will have another one here by lunchtime. Evidently the town has a great deal of its liquid funds tied up in this festival, so the show must go on."

"Did George actually say that?" I asked him skeptically.

"No, that was Cassandra's take on it. The mayor brought her with him to the clock for my report, if you can believe that."

It was apparent that the chief didn't like the mayor's new girlfriend. If Chief Grant felt that she was interfering with his ability to do his job, I couldn't say that I blamed him, but Cassandra hadn't really been in town long enough to make waves.

"Do you at least know who the man was?" I asked him.

"I'm sorry to say that I don't. His prints don't show up on any of our databases, so that means that he's never been arrested, served in the military, or been in government service," the chief said.

"I've never been any of those things, either," I said gently.

"Neither have a ton of other people. It's just making him hard to identify."

"Didn't he carry a wallet on him? It's hard to imagine someone leaving the house without some kind of identification or credit card on them in this day and age."

"His pockets were empty, all except for a smooth little rock the size of your thumb."

"Odd," I said. "Were there any clues in his clothing?"

"The labels had all been cut out of them a long time ago," the police chief said. "We're working on it, but this one's going to take some time."

"I'm sorry. You must be frustrated on all kinds of levels."

"It seems to be part of my job most days," Chief Grant said

as he pushed the empty cup away. "That was a mighty fine donut hole. The icing was a particularly nice touch."

"I'm glad you enjoyed it," I said. "Keep me posted, okay?"

"I will if I can," he said. "Suzanne, you're not going to dig into this too, are you?"

I shook my head. "No, sir; not me. I'm smart enough to know that I'm way over my head with this one. It sounds as though it's going to take all of your resources to figure this one out."

He seemed mollified by my statement. "Okay then."

I suddenly had second thoughts about what I'd just said. "Chief, I reserve the right to change my mind at any time. You realize that, don't you?" I added a grin to take some of the edge off my disclaimer.

After shoving some money at me across the counter, the chief stood and smiled as he admired our other offerings in the case. "I've known you a long time, Suzanne. I would be shocked if you didn't dig into this at one point, so don't feel like you're disappointing me." He pointed to the decorated donut holes one last time as he added, "I really do like these a lot."

"I'll be sure and tell Emma," I said.

After the police chief was gone, my assistant came out and smiled. "Did I just spot our police chief eating one of our donut creations?"

"He said to tell you they were great," I said. "You could have come out and spoken with him yourself, you know."

"I would have, but you two looked as though you were having a serious conversation."

I'd debated telling Emma about the man I'd found on the dunking-booth platform when she'd first come in, but something had made me hesitate. If I didn't do it right now, I knew that it might cause problems later. "Emma, there's something I need to tell you."

"I'm listening," she said absently. She was a little distracted as she tried to right a donut-hole eyeball that had slipped out of alignment with the others.

"I found a dead man perched on the dunking-booth bench this morning on my break."

Emma looked at me curiously for a moment to see if I was joking, but when she realized that I wasn't, she frowned at me. "And you're just telling me this now *why*, exactly?"

"I'm not sure. You were so happy when you came in, I suppose I just didn't want to ruin the mood," I said, which was at least partially true.

"I get that. Plus, you didn't want me calling my dad right away. I understand. You didn't want him to print what you'd uncovered in tomorrow's newspaper."

"Emma, there's nothing to print just yet beside the fact that I found a body. The police chief doesn't even know if he died of natural causes or if he was murdered. Shoot, he hasn't even been able to identify the body yet."

"Are you saying that you didn't recognize him?" she asked me.

"No, I've never seen him before in my life."

After a moment, she asked me timidly, "If it's going to be a problem I won't do it, but do you mind if I call my dad?"

"I don't mind a bit, but I don't know what you can tell him. At this point, nobody knows anything about what happened this morning."

"That's what Dad's going to run with, unless I miss my guess," she said. "*Mystery Man Dies Under Extraordinary Circumstances*. Doesn't that sound like one of his headlines to you?"

"Are you sure you haven't been writing them for him?" I

asked her with a slight smile. "It sounds exactly like one of his banners."

"No, they're all his, but he's got a certain distinctive style, wouldn't you say?"

"I would wholeheartedly agree with that," I said, trying to be as diplomatic as I could.

Emma took out her phone and called him on the spot. After a few moments, she said, "No. No. I'll ask her, but I'm already telling you that the answer is no." Putting her phone to her shoulder, Emma asked me, "You wouldn't care to give a firsthand account of what you saw this morning to the newspaper editor, would you?"

"No comment," I said with a grin.

"That's what I told him you'd say, but hey, at least I tried," Emma replied, smiling right back at me. "She said no comment, Dad. Yep. That's it."

Before she could hang up, I said, "Emma. One second."

"Hang on, Dad," she said to him before turning to me. "What's up?"

"Have him ask the chief for a photo of the dead man's face. If he runs it in the paper, maybe someone will recognize him."

"Do you think the chief would ever let that happen?" Emma asked me.

I had a hunch Chief Grant would take every bit of help he could get, even from Ray Blake. "The way I see it, what could it hurt to ask?"

After my assistant gave Ray my suggestion, she said, "Okay. I've got to go. Love you, too, Dad. Bye."

After Emma hung up, I said, "Thanks for looking out for me with your father."

"Always," she said. "And thank *you* for giving Dad the idea of running a photo of the dead man."

I wasn't about to tell her that I had ulterior motives. "Happy to help."

Emma scanned the display cases and smiled. "I can't wait to see how everybody else reacts to these treats."

"Stick around," I said as I pointed to a few people milling around outside waiting for me to officially open the shop for the day.

"Okay," she said with a grin. "Maybe we should decorate the window too since we're getting into the spirit of Fright Week. I still have some of that special glass paint left over from Christmas."

As I went to let our waiting customers in, I said, "I don't think red and green will match our motif, do you?"

"Oh, we've got all kinds of colors in the kit to cover all of the major holidays," she said. "I think there are even a few stencils in there, too. I seem to remember a spider and some webbing and a jack o'lantern."

"Why not?" I asked with a shrug. In for a penny, in for a pound, after all. "Go ahead and get started."

"Excellent. This is going to be fun," she said with glee. Emma believed that if something was worth doing, it was worth overdoing, and her enthusiasm was catching.

I opened the door and stood aside as three of my regular customers walked inside.

Their reactions to our decorating were mixed, but I was fine with that. I'd learned a long time ago that it was impossible to please everyone. That was why if I liked something, and Emma didn't show a strong disapproval of the idea, I usually just went ahead and did whatever I fancied. It made life a lot more fun than doing everything by committee and hoping not to offend anyone as my main objective in life. After all, no one opens a donut shop for the money. If you can't enjoy the process, there's no reason to get out of bed in the morning.

I certainly wasn't expecting my next visitor to the donut shop after the first crowd left, at least not in the state he was in. "It's not raining out, is it, Jake?" I asked my husband as he walked into Donut Hearts. His hair was wet, as well as his shirt and quite a bit of his pants.

"First of all, don't panic, Suzanne. I've got everything under control," he said as he held his hands out toward me.

"Okay, now I'm officially worried," I said. "What's going on?"

He frowned for a moment before he spoke. "I ran into a slight complication at the cottage a few minutes ago."

"Based on your appearance, I have to ask you this. Don't take offense, but how slight?"

Instead of answering my question directly, he asked me, "Do you remember how you wanted me to hang that picture in our bedroom?"

I'd found a print of a waterfall in the North Carolina Mountains that had looked soothing, and on a lark, I'd bought it. Jake had insisted that he hang it himself, but that had been three weeks ago. "I remember. What happened? Did it somehow magically start leaking water?"

"Of course not," he said. "The wall behind it did, though," he added glumly.

"How is that even possible?" I asked.

"It appears that the main water line for the upstairs bathroom passes directly behind the wall where I drove a nail to hang your picture," he said, "but like I said, don't panic. Everything's going to be fine. Better than fine, actually."

"Is the water *still* leaking?" I asked him as I started to take off my apron so I could assess the damage personally.

"No, of course not. I got it stopped in hardly any time at all. Or so I thought."

"There's more to this story, isn't there?" I asked him, getting more alarmed by the moment.

"It's an old cottage, Suzanne. When I tried to turn the water off at the main shutoff, the knob broke off in my hand. That's when the real flood started."

How long was he going to prolong my misery? "Jake, I can't take this news in bits and pieces. Just give me the worst of it, okay?"

"I told you, we're all good. We got the water shut off at the street in no time at all," Jake said, doing his best to reassure me and failing miserably at it.

"Who exactly is 'we'?"

"Phillip happened to stop by to ask me my opinion about a cold case he's been digging into. Between the two of us, we got the cover off the water main and shut it off from the source. The cottage is drying out even as we speak. Like I said, there's no cause for alarm."

"I'm not so sure about that. Did you call a plumber to take care of it?"

"I'm not about to waste good money on something I can do myself," Jake said proudly. As a state police investigator, he was the tops. As a plumber, I suspected not so much.

"We can afford to bring in an expert, Jake. Why don't you call somebody? I'm sure Momma knows somebody good." My mother owned quite a bit of real estate, both buildings and property, in and around April Springs, so I knew that she'd have access to someone immediately, which was apparently exactly what we needed.

"I'm sure she does, but we're not going to need her contacts to fix this. Phillip has agreed to help me. Between the two of us, we should have it knocked out in one day, two at the most."

"What are we supposed to do for water in the meantime?" I

asked him, feeling my voice getting shriller and shriller by the moment.

"I've already covered that. We're staying with your mother and Phillip. Like I said, it won't take us any time at all."

"Jake, you do realize that just because they fix problems in an hour on television doesn't mean that you'll be able to." My husband had become a great fan of the DIY channels lately, and he often remarked how simple it all looked.

"Suzanne, how hard could it be?" he asked me.

"Harder than you think," I said softly.

Apparently his mind was made up, though. "I know it's not going to be *that* easy, but honestly, we can do it. Phillip and I are both retired cops, and we've handled situations a lot dicier than this. Between the two of us, we should be able to handle it without a sweat."

"If you two were investigating a case, I'd have no doubt in your abilities," I said, trying to keep myself calm. "I'm just worried that this is out of your realm of expertise."

"You worry too much," he said as he kissed my nose. "Now I've got to go. Phillip is waiting for me. I'll see you later."

"I can't talk you out of this, can I?" I asked one last time.

"No, ma'am. You'll see. It'll be a snap." With that, Jake snapped his fingers to demonstrate how easy he thought the task would be. Before leaving, he pointed to the display cases. "I love the new donuts. You should let folks know what you're doing."

Before he could go, I knew there was something I needed to tell him. I'd been putting it off because I hadn't wanted him to worry about me. "Jake, I found a body this morning in front of the town clock, perched on the dunking-booth bench."

"I was wondering when you'd get around to telling me about that," he said with a nod. "Phillip already knew about it, and he told me first thing. I'm sorry you had to see that."

"What do you think happened to the man?" I asked.

"I don't know, but I have as much confidence in Chief Grant to solve it as I do in Phillip and myself to fix that leak in no time."

His response wasn't exactly inspiring, but I kept my reservations to myself.

After all, maybe he was right.

I wasn't going to hold my breath, though.

I knew that I needed to pack enough clothes for the long haul when I got off work. Hopefully I'd still be able to get into my cottage by then, but I was already having my doubts. What fresh madness would the two former cops create in their efforts to fix an "easy" problem?

Only time would tell.

In the meantime, I had donuts to sell.

CHAPTER 3

"ARE THOSE REALLY EYEBALLS?" PAIGE Hill asked as she surveyed the donut display case.

"Well, not really, but that's what they're supposed to look like. Do you like them?" I asked her.

"Like them? I *love* them. Can I buy them all?"

"Sure, why not?" I asked as I grabbed a few boxes and carefully placed our inventory inside them. "That's why they are there."

"I agree with you, but I went into a donut chain in Asheville once and saw that they had peanut donuts for sale. There were eight left, so I bought them out. You would have thought I was robbing them! Three different employees scolded me for wiping out their inventory of peanut donuts, each making a point to tell me that if I knew that I wanted that many, I could and should call ahead the day before so they could be ready for me. Can you imagine that? What would you do if someone came in with a few hundred dollars and offered to buy out your inventory for the day?"

"Let's see. I'd probably go home early, take a long shower, and then grab a nice long nap," I said with a grin.

"But would you chastise the customer for buying your donuts?" she asked as I took her money and made change.

"Are you kidding? I *dream* about customers like that. What are you going to do with these? Besides eat them, I mean."

"I'm going to put them out for my customers. They're going

24

to fit perfectly in my display," she said with a grin. "I've been revisiting some of my favorite old horror novels this week in honor of Fright Week. I've planned readings and events all week based on the idea that everyone loves to be frightened every now and then. Do you like scary books, Suzanne?"

"I used to love them when I was younger, but as I've grown older, I've become a huge cozy-mystery fan. If it weren't for the murders, I wouldn't mind living in some of the small towns I've read about."

"To each her own," Paige said with a shrug. "That's why there are so many books. There's something for just about everyone," she said. "Are you making more of these eyeball donut holes tomorrow?"

"Why, did you want to go ahead and place an order today?" I asked her with a grin.

"That's the problem, isn't it? I rarely know what I want at any particular moment, let alone what my cravings might be tomorrow."

"Well, feel free to come in and buy me out anytime you'd like," I told Paige as I held the door open for her. I couldn't imagine a shopkeeper not being excited about selling out her supply of anything. After all, it meant more money in the till and a move one step closer to making a profit that day, and that was ultimately one of the reasons we were in business, wasn't it? Sure, I loved making people happy with my sweet treats, but I also loved making a living while I was doing it. Why couldn't I do both, though?

"I'm going to take off now, if that's okay with you," Emma said a little later as she came out of the kitchen. "The dishes are done, at least for now."

"Thanks so much. The window looks great, by the way."

My assistant had outdone herself using the cobweb and spider stencils to the max, giving Donut Hearts a decidedly Halloween feel inside and out now.

"Sweet. When I come in tomorrow, do you mind if I bring in some cobwebs for the inside? We could really do wonders in here with a few well-placed spider webs."

"Okay, but don't make it too creepy. We have a lot of little kids come into the shop, and I don't want to scare them off. Try to keep it a bit whimsical, okay?"

"I think that ship has sailed with the donut-hole eyeballs, but I get your point," Emma replied with a grin. "See you later."

"Bye," I said.

As my assistant walked out of the shop, George Morris and Cassandra Lane came in. The mayor and his girlfriend were both smiling broadly. Given my earlier discovery, I hadn't expected that reaction from them. George was usually a gruff-looking man, an ex-cop who didn't stand for much nonsense, but it was amazing to see his transformation in Cassandra's presence. The elegant blonde brought out a side of my friend that I loved seeing. Even in jeans and a plain blouse, Cassandra had a presence about her that must have made her a fierce foe in the courtroom. She seemed to command attention whenever she was present.

"I love the window!" she said gleefully. "You're really getting into the spirit of Fright Week, Suzanne."

"The donuts look good, too," George added.

"You just missed the donut-hole eyeballs," I said. "We made them in blue, green, and brown. They're a real hoot."

"Are you teasing, or did you really make them?" Cassandra asked.

"They were here all right, but Paige Hill bought the last few we had left. Tomorrow we'll have more, though."

"Excellent. I'm glad to see that at least *some* of the shop owners are getting into the spirit of the season," Cassandra said.

"I thought everyone was participating. Paige just told me that she's celebrating all week with horror-novel readings and events, and Emily Hargraves has Cow, Spots, and Moose dressed up in their finest Halloween attire. As a matter of fact, they are wearing different costumes every day. Emily had plenty to choose from, since she's been dressing her stuffed animals up for years."

"I know. We just left her. They are all dressed as ghosts today. What a cute gimmick she's got," Cassandra said.

"It's a lot more than just a gimmick," I said. "Emily's one of the shrewdest marketers around. She knows how much of a draw her three childhood pals are, and she maximizes the interest to draw people into her newsstand."

"Max was there with her," George said lightly, referring to Emily's current boyfriend and my ex-husband.

"It's awfully early for him to be up and about, isn't it?" I asked with a grin. When Max and I had been married, it had been a rare day that he'd been up before noon, but evidently a great many things had changed since he'd started dating my friend.

"He didn't seem to mind. Emily has done a wonderful job with the newsstand. She's even got a contest going to guess the number of candy skulls in a big glass jar. The winner gets the candy, the jar, and a ten-dollar gift certificate to her shop," Cassandra said. "Are you planning on running any promotions here, besides the decorations and donuts, I mean?"

"We're holding a donut-decorating competition," I said as I explained the different categories and age groups. Emma and I decided on doing spookiest, funniest, and most creative for each of our divisions. Why not spread the fun around even more? "They'll be held at different times, all leading up to the grand finale on Halloween morning, an All Star decorating challenge with all of the division winners vying for the grand prize! Who wouldn't want to win a donut a week for an entire year?"

"That sounds perfect," Cassandra said. In a softer voice, she asked, "Suzanne, do you think you might be able to speak with Gabby about her participation?"

Gabby Williams was my gruff neighbor in business. She ran ReNEWed, a gently used clothing shop that sported the best fashion April Springs had to offer. It didn't really surprise me that she'd chosen not to participate in the festivities. "I'm not sure why you're asking me. I don't have any more influence with Gabby than the mayor does," I said.

"We both know better than that," George said. "Please, Suzanne? It would mean a lot to me. To us, I mean."

It was odd for George to care so much about a festival, but then again, it was clear that he was trying to make Cassandra happy. "I'll see what I can do," I said with a bit of reluctance in my voice. "Do you have a minute, Mr. Mayor? I want to talk to you about what happened earlier this morning."

"Are you talking about that poor unfortunate man you found?" Cassandra asked, chiming in, even though she hadn't been invited into the conversation.

"Yes," I said, looking at her briefly and hoping that she'd get the hint that I wanted a moment with the mayor alone.

"Sadly, life and death go hand in hand, don't they? We all have our own time, don't we? Dying is just a natural part of the process of living. There's no reason we should halt the festivities because of it."

"Have you heard something that I haven't?" I asked her. "I didn't know that he died of natural causes."

"What else *could* it be?" she asked. "According to the police chief, there were no signs of trauma present on the body when he examined it."

"Cassandra, you're an attorney. Surely you must realize

that just because there were no overt signs of murder, it doesn't necessarily mean that it was a natural death."

"Suzanne," George jumped in, "she's right. Unfortunately, it happens all of the time. Your problem is that you've seen too many bodies over the years. You're starting to see murder everywhere." Before I could protest, he continued, "We've decided that unless there's evidence to the contrary that the death wasn't from natural causes, Fright Week is going to go on as planned. We have too much invested in it to shut it down on rumor and speculation."

"Is that the mayor talking, or the event planner's boyfriend?" I asked a little pointedly. It was the relationship George and I had developed over the years, but Cassandra looked startled by my bluntness in her presence.

"The mayor," George said stiffly.

Perhaps I had been a little harsh with him, but before I could smooth things out with him, Cassandra put her arm in his and led him to the door. "Let's go, Mr. Mayor. We have more stops to make before our meeting. Good day, Suzanne."

"George," I called out, still hoping to have a word with him in private.

"It'll have to be later, Suzanne," the mayor said, and then they were gone.

I knew that everyone in town loved Cassandra and her overwhelming presence, but sometimes she could be a little tough to take. If George had been making the decision alone, I had a hunch Fright Week would be over before it had a chance to get started, but with Cassandra whispering in his ear, it was a whole different matter. Then again, maybe they were right. The stranger I'd found might have died from natural causes, no matter how odd the way I'd discovered him might have been.

Still, to die on a dunk tank bench wearing a Halloween mask was not ordinary by any definition of the word.

The decorated donut treats sold better than I'd expected, and by closing time, I was left with one donut, a rare event for me. I almost always made more than I needed on the theory that I'd rather have too many on hand than run out of things to sell in the course of the morning. The lone survivor was a pumpkin spice cake donut that we'd decorated a little too heavily with black icing. I couldn't bring myself to throw it away, so, after looking around and seeing that I was alone, I ate it myself.

The icing might not have been too appealing to the eye, but it was delightful to the taste. Glancing in the mirror to brush away any crumbs that might be present, I noticed that my teeth had taken on a decidedly dark tone from the icing. Scrubbing them with a tissue helped, but it wasn't until after I'd brushed thoroughly that I was satisfied with the result. In the future I would definitely have to back off on the food coloring or use less icing, so it was a valuable lesson.

Since Emma had done some of the dishes while she'd been there earlier, it made cleanup easier for me, and I was out of the donut shop in record time. After dropping off the deposit at the bank, I circled back to the cottage to see if, by any miracle, Jake and Phillip had finished their home improvement project.

"What happened here?"

"Take a deep breath and try to relax, Suzanne. It's not as bad as it looks," Jake said, doing his best to calm me down and failing miserably at it.

"It couldn't be any worse, could it?" I had been expecting a little hole in the wall of the bedroom, but when I arrived, I was faced with nearly an entire section of plaster ripped down, exposing the studs, the wiring, and the punctured plumbing. "I thought it was just a little leak."

"The truth is, it's lucky that it happened," Phillip chimed in, trying to rush to my husband's defense.

"If this is lucky, I'd hate to see what unlucky looks like," I replied.

"The thing is, we found a minor electrical problem we need to address, too," Jake said.

"What do you two think you're doing? Will you at least admit now that it's time to call in a professional?"

"What, and get ripped off by their high prices?" Jake asked. "I've seen this exact same work done a thousand times on television. Sometimes you have to take a project a few steps back before you can move forward."

"Do you honestly call this a *few* steps?" I asked, incredulous at how much destruction these two men had accomplished in such a short period of time.

"You sound just like Dot did a little bit ago," Phillip said, referring to my mother.

"*Momma's* seen this?" I asked.

"She came by to check on our progress less than an hour ago," Phillip admitted.

"Please tell me that she at least insisted on calling someone in to look at this," I said, hoping that my mother had been a rational voice in this sea of insanity.

"She was pushing for it at first, but she finally agreed to give us twenty-four hours to keep digging into this," Phillip said.

"There were a few conditions," Jake added a little sullenly. "You realize that we didn't have to agree to those, don't you?" my husband told his partner in crime.

"Sir, you clearly don't know my wife. If we hadn't, she would have had a full crew over here before Suzanne even got home."

"Tell me the conditions she placed on you," I said, doing my best to keep my voice calm and level. What had Momma been thinking, giving these two maniacs free rein on the cottage repair? At the stage it was in now, it almost looked as though it needed to be torn down and rebuilt.

"The first thing we had to agree to do was to turn off the power at the main breaker," Phillip said. "She expressed a fear that we might electrocute ourselves."

"Well, I suppose that's something," I conceded. At least that way they wouldn't end up killing themselves in the process of trying to save a little money. "What else?"

"We have to leave the water off, too. I've got to tell you, it's making it pretty inconvenient not having water or electricity here," Jake said.

"I'm sure you'll both find a way to live with it. Is that it?"

"We're not supposed to do anything structural to the cottage either, like taking down walls or things like that," Jake said, almost sounding as though he resented that particular condition.

"Your mother said that she was worried about the old place, but I'm not sure how much we can do, given the conditions she demanded from us," Phillip said.

"It's not so bad. We'll do what we planned to all along. After we fix the plumbing leak, we'll rewire some of this, and then we'll get it all buttoned back up, nice and neat," Jake said as he slapped his partner on the back. "We should have it finished by dinnertime."

That was one of the loftiest goals I'd ever heard in my life. "By dinner? As in tonight?"

"Well, by nine o'clock, anyway," Jake said, conceding that maybe he'd been a little too enthusiastic in his prediction of completion.

"Tell her the final condition," Phillip urged my husband.

"Your mother gets to bring in a licensed contractor to inspect our work after we're finished," Jake said almost sullenly.

"And we can't plaster anything over, either. I'm not even sure if what she's agreed to let us do is worth doing at this point," Phillip lamented.

"Come on. There's still a *lot* left for us." Jake turned back to me. "Suzanne, you should probably pack a bag for tonight, just in case. We're going to be hard at work here, so there's no telling when we're going to get finished up."

"Should I pack something for you, too? Forget I even asked. I'm going to pack a bag for you, too," I said, answering the question I'd just asked him without waiting for confirmation.

"Our clothes aren't in there," Jake said softly as I started toward the dresser.

"What do you mean?"

"We didn't want everything to get dusty, so we moved it all up into the upstairs bedroom," Jake said. The thought of my stepfather handling my clothing was more than I could take, and what was more, my husband realized it. "Don't worry, I moved your clothes myself."

Thank goodness for small favors. I suddenly realized that it might be better if I just got out of there before I said something that I might end up regretting. After all, most of the damage to the cottage had already been done.

Hadn't it?

As I started upstairs to gather our clothing, Jake turned to Phillip and said, "Don't do anything for a second. I'll be right back."

"Jake, I wouldn't dream of moving forward without you," my stepfather said, clearly planning to do just that once my husband was out of sight.

Furthermore, Jake knew it, too. "Just in case you're tempted, I'll take the flashlight with me so Suzanne doesn't trip on the stairs," he said with a broad grin. Without its illumination, the bedroom was more than just a little dark, given that clouds had populated the sky and were now putting a gloom on everything.

"Fine. I'll just sit here in the dark and wait for you," Phillip said sullenly.

"I won't be long," Jake said.

My husband's grin vanished as he saw the look of disapproval on my face.

"Is something wrong?" he asked me.

"Jake, are you really going to try to tackle this yourself?"

"Come on. What could it hurt? You've been telling me for months that I needed a hobby."

"True, but I didn't expect it to come from the complete demolition of our home," I said as I entered my old bedroom upstairs.

I'd been expecting a haphazard pile of mixed clothing strewn across the bed, but I was relieved to see that my meticulous husband had made certain that everything was folded neatly and organized on the bedspread. I supposed in the scheme of things that was something positive to take from the experience, anyway. Since we kept our overnight bags in the upstairs closet anyway, I packed two bags for us quickly, and then I was ready to go.

"That's way too many clothes for just one night," Jake protested.

"Humor me," I said.

"I get it," Jake said with a smile. "After all, you might want to change outfits more than once, am I right?"

My husband had clearly lost his mind, but there was nothing much I could do but just smile and nod in agreement. "Sure. Why not? That's why I'm taking so much."

Once I had the bags packed, I started to pick them up when Jake hugged me tightly and gave me a solid kiss before releasing me.

"Thanks for letting me take a swing at this," he said, and I could see how happy he was to be doing something productive, or at least what he considered productive.

"Just try not to do *too* much more demolition today, okay?" I asked.

"I'm not making any promises," he said with a smile.

I wasn't going to budge on that though, no matter how cute he looked. "Jake. Promise me."

"Okay, I promise, but you've been telling me for months that you wished the front window looking out onto the park was larger."

"Don't you dare!" I said firmly before I saw his grin.

"I'm just kidding, Suzanne. Come on. Loosen up."

I knew any response to that would be the wrong one, so I just gave his cheek a quick kiss, and then I said, "Just be careful, okay?"

"You know I will," he replied.

Once we were downstairs again, my husband walked me out onto the front porch. Storm clouds were definitely brewing, and I wondered how they would impact the evening's Fright Week activities. Then again, it had been scary enough inside my cottage without the threat of an impending storm.

As I stowed the overnight bags into the Jeep, I knew that I needed to speak with Momma. As much as I appreciated her putting limits on our husbands, I believed that she should have stopped them altogether. Jake and Phillip might be able to steamroll one of us at any given time, but I knew that if I could get Momma on my side, they wouldn't stand a chance, and we'd have professionals tackling the job instead of two well-intentioned but seriously undertrained amateurs.

CHAPTER 4

I WAS DETERMINED TO SPEAK WITH Momma immediately, but then I saw Grace's car parked in her driveway, so I pulled the Jeep in beside it to see what she was doing home before noon. My best friend pretty much made her own hours working as a supervisor for a large cosmetics company, but I was still surprised to find her home at midday.

Grace answered the door looking decidedly frazzled. "Hey, Suzanne. What's up?"

"That's what I want to know," I said. "Isn't that a little bit of overaccessorizing, even for you?"

My best friend had three scarves draped over one shoulder, looking as though she was getting ready for the dance of a thousand veils, or three scarves, whatever the case might be. "What? Oh, these," she said as she realized she had them on. "Yes. I'm packing, and I don't know what to take. I've got a meeting with my boss's boss in Atlanta."

"Is something amiss?" I asked her.

"No. Maybe. I don't know. They do this every now and then. I've been told that this meeting is to gauge my thoughts on a new product rollout, but who knows what the real reason is? All I know is that I need to be there by seven for dinner, and I'm not even close to finishing packing."

"Need any help?" I asked her, though I knew that Grace was as meticulous at packing as she was at dressing.

"I can handle that, but you can keep me company if you have a few minutes to spare," she said.

"For you? Always," I said.

"Come on in, then."

I followed my best friend into her bedroom, and I saw that most of her work was already done. She'd laid out five outfits and their accouterments. "I don't know why I'm bringing any of these at all," she said as she put the scarves back into her closet. Closing up her bags, she said, "That's got to be good enough. I'm running dangerously low on time." Grace paused a moment, and then she added, "I heard you found a new body this morning."

"I did, but it appears that no one believes there was anything suspicious about it," I said.

"Why on earth not? It was hanging from the town clock, wasn't it?" Grace asked as I grabbed one bag while she got the other.

"Where on earth did you hear that?"

"Sam at the gas station. I had to fill up my tank for the drive," she said.

"For your information, the man was sitting on the bench of the dunking tank wearing a pumpkin mask," I said.

"And *that's* not suspicious to Stephen?" Grace asked incredulously. "I know my boyfriend can be thick at times, but that screams murder, doesn't it?"

"Don't be too hard on him. He's doing the best he can. I agree with you, and I suspect the police chief does as well. I believe it at least bears looking into, but the mayor is strong-arming the chief into putting it on the back burner so it doesn't interfere with Fright Week."

"I'm guessing that Cassandra Lane is behind that," she said. "Is it just me, or is she exerting an unusually high amount of influence on George lately?"

"He might be a *little* too eager to please her," I conceded, though I agreed with Grace wholeheartedly.

"A little? I can't believe an ex-cop like George would just blow this off for the sake of a made-up festival."

"At least the chief is *trying* to investigate," I said, "with or without the mayor's full support."

"I'm just sorry that I'm going out of town. I bet between the two of us we'd be able to figure out what really happened to that man. Are you and Jake going to dig into it?"

"Unfortunately, Jake and Phillip have their hands full at the moment. They've decided to renovate the cottage."

"What? When did this happen?" Grace asked, pausing on her way to the front door.

"The plan was initiated when Jake tried to hang a picture and hit a water supply line for the upstairs bathroom in the process," I said.

"And you're going to just let them wreck your place?"

"I'm on my way to Momma's to straighten things out," I said as we got outside.

"That's smart. She's the best person in the world I know of to have your back."

"Besides you, you mean," I told her with a grin as I handed her the bag I'd been carrying.

"Of course," Grace said with a grin. After her bags were safely stowed away, she hugged me as she added, "Just don't go trying to investigate this one alone."

"What makes you think that I'd ever do that?" I asked her.

"Come on, Suzanne. I've known you too long not to believe that it's at least a possibility."

She had a point, but I didn't have to concede it. Instead, I decided to ignore it completely. "Have a safe trip," I said.

"I will, but I hate missing Fright Week. It sounds like a load of fun."

"I'm not sure how much you'll be missing. Call me if you need to chat."

"Right back at you," she said.

After Grace was gone, I got into my Jeep and headed to Momma's house.

Hopefully I could get to the bottom of her decision not to stop the men dead in their tracks.

It was a poor choice of words, but the sentiment was real enough.

"Can you believe those two maniacs we married?" I asked Momma as she answered the door. She'd given me walk-in privileges the moment she'd moved into her new place, but I still had a hard time using them.

"Good afternoon to you, too, Suzanne," Momma said with a grin.

"Sorry. Hi. I can't believe you didn't shut them down on the spot."

"I considered it briefly, but they make a good point."

I looked to see if there were any obvious physical signs that my mother had lost her mind, but I couldn't see any. "In what way *possible* could that be true?"

"I've been worrying about the wiring and plumbing in that place for years," Momma said. "I always put it off though, just waiting for a good opportunity to do it over correctly and bring everything up to code."

"And you honestly think that those two amateurs can do it?" I asked.

She laughed at the very thought of it. "Of course not. They are so far in over their heads they can't even see it."

"Then why indulge them?" I asked her.

"Suzanne, if we do as you suggest and shut them down right now, they will both go to their graves believing that they were capable of the job, but we stood in their way. However, if we let them see just how wrong they are, then I'm guessing that the do-it-yourself projects will come to an end. I don't know about Jake, but Phillip believes he can do anything after watching one episode of a home improvement show on television. Why not let them realize that it's not as easy as it looks?"

"The work still needs to be done though, and frankly, we don't have the budget for it, Momma," I admitted.

"That's the beauty of it, though," she said. "I've been looking for something to get you two for Christmas. What better gift than updated plumbing and wiring?"

"Well, for one thing, it's quite a bit more than the sweaters we were going to get you and Phillip," I said.

"I love sweaters," she said with a grin.

"I know that, but I still can't let you do it. It's too much."

Momma's smile brightened even more. "What if I told you that it would be an inexpensive undertaking, Suzanne?"

"I'd say that you've been watching too much television, too."

"Not when you've heard the backstory. I bought a few houses in Union Square to flip last month, and the contractor I was using overbought on everything. He wasn't padding his bill. He just overestimated what he'd need for the jobs, and I found myself with wiring and plumbing materials that can't be returned and nowhere to use them. They've already been written off as a loss for that particular business venture, so why not use them ourselves?"

"Be that as it may, labor is going to be tremendous," I said, "not to mention the plasterwork after it's all finished."

"Don't worry about the labor," she said. "He's already agreed to do the job at cost. You see, he's an excellent builder. He's just not a great businessman. The entire job will be done at a fraction of what you'd normally have to pay for it, and I for one know that I'll sleep better at night knowing that everything at the cottage has been updated."

"Okay, I see how it makes sense, and I appreciate the gesture, but if that's all true, why not get him started right now instead of letting Jake and Phillip tackle it first, their pride notwithstanding?" Before she answered the question, I suddenly knew the answer. "He can't start the job for twenty-four hours, can he? That's why you gave them free rein until then."

"What harm could it do, especially since I warned them not to do anything structural?" Momma asked me. "Don't you see the beauty of it?"

"I suppose so, but it's not going to be a very happy few days even *after* we replace them, is it?"

"Oh, they'll be fine once they see the reality of the situation. Do you mind staying with us while the work is being finished? It could be fun having you live with me again."

"As kind as the gesture is, the last time we cohabitated, neither one of us had husbands, remember?" I asked.

"So much the better. Now don't be so gloomy. It's all going to work out just fine in the end."

"If you say so," I said, not fully believing it myself.

"Consider it settled, then. Now, tell me about finding that body this morning. The entire town is fussing about it."

"There's not much to tell," I said, Grace's earlier words still haunting me a little. Was the chief allowing the mayor to sweep the homicide under the rug for the sake of Fright Week? Surely someone needed to investigate what had really happened. Waiting for the coroner's report could take some time, and in the meantime, leads could get stone cold. Maybe I *should* investigate, but I couldn't do it alone. With Grace gone and Jake tied up with renovations, where did that leave me?

"Suzanne? Are you still with me?" Momma said, bringing me back to the moment.

"Sorry," I said, focusing my attention back on her. I did have *one* investigating partner left, and she was standing right in front of me. Momma had helped me investigate my great-aunt Jean's murder, and she'd proved to be a good ally. But would she do it again, when there was nothing as personal at stake as there had been before? "I spaced out for a minute. Did you just say something else?"

"I said that the two of us need to figure out what happened to that poor man if no one else is going to," Momma said.

"I thought you were finished with investigating murder," I reminded her.

"We don't even know if it *was* murder yet," she said. "Besides, I hate to see this ignored just because that poor man wasn't from April Springs. Are you sure you didn't recognize him?"

"I can honestly say that I'd never seen him before in my life," I said.

"Tell me about what you saw this morning, and try not to leave anything out," Momma said, my luggage temporarily forgotten for the moment. I wished I'd taken a photo of the dead man once we'd gotten the mask off, but there hadn't been any way for me to do it without Officer Bradley noticing, and that was a fight I hadn't wanted to have at the time. Still, I could describe him well enough, and after I recounted what I'd seen, I did my best to paint a mental picture for my mother.

"That's a pretty vivid image you've described," she said after I was finished. "So, we are in search of who might have killed the scruffy moon-faced man."

"I'm not so sure we should describe him that way," I said, thinking that it sounded kind of harsh upon hearing my mother say it.

"Don't worry. We'll put it more delicately when we're interviewing people," Momma said dismissively.

"Who exactly are we going to interview? The only people usually out that time of morning are me and Stevie Marks." Stevie, a high school junior, had taken over the newspaper delivery route for Ray Blake's newspaper after the former carrier had retired and moved to Florida to stay with his brother.

"Do you think there's a chance he saw anything?" Momma asked.

"I'd be surprised. The poor boy is barely able to keep his head up at that time of day. I don't know how he doesn't wreck his car along his route, not that it would be easy to tell if there were any new dings, dents, or scratches on that heap he drives. We could always ask him, though."

"I'm sure Chief Grant has already quizzed him," Momma said, "if he even bothered to dig that deeply. I need to have a chat with George about where his real duties lie as mayor."

I was certain that conversation wouldn't turn out well for anyone. "Momma, maybe you can hold off scolding him until after we've done some investigating ourselves. It might pay to be diplomatic for the moment, given that we're about to conduct our own investigation without any official permission or approval."

"Perhaps you are right," Momma said, which told me that she'd make up her own mind, so there was no use in me continuing. "Where might we find Stevie at this time of day? Is he in school?"

"No, he only goes half a day. He should be delivering groceries about now. I don't know how many jobs he has, but I have no idea when he sleeps."

"He certainly sounds like an enterprising young man. Suzanne, you don't have your groceries delivered, do you?"

"No, I couldn't afford it, but I let Stevie put a flyer up in the donut shop when he first got started."

"What is he going to do with the money he is acquiring? Does he plan to use it for college?" Momma asked.

"Not Stevie. He wants to be an entrepreneur. I suppose in a very real way he already is. The last I heard, he delivers papers early in the morning, goes to school, and then, after he finishes his grocery deliveries for the day, he tutors students in math and science."

"I'm looking forward to meeting him," Momma said.

I handed her my phone. "Then call the grocery store and place an order. There's a thirty-dollar minimum, but you should be able to meet it easily."

Momma frowned, ignoring my phone. "Why don't we just go speak with him without going through the ruse of buying groceries?"

"Momma, we can't just corner a high school boy and start grilling him. However, if he's here making a delivery, it's only natural if we should ask him a few questions. Oh, if you pay the ten-dollar premium, he'll have them here within half an hour."

"I suppose I could find enough things to make it worth my while," Momma said. When she was ready, I gave her the number. It wasn't that I had a particularly good memory, but Stevie's number was easy to remember, since it included my birthday in a prominent spot.

After Momma placed her order, she said, "Now we wait."

"In the meantime, let's talk about who else we can ask after we talk to Stevie," I said.

"I'm not at all certain there *is* anyone else we can speak with," Momma said. "But I have another idea. Why don't we go to the largest source of gossip and rumor in all of April Springs?"

"The beauty shop?" I asked her, referring to Cutnip.

"That's good, but it's not perfect. I've found that the Boxcar Grill has a wider variety of older men, and it has been my experience that they gossip more than women ever dreamed of

44

doing. Do you think Trish would mind if we mine her customer base?"

"If we include her in the investigation, she'll be ecstatic," I said.

"Then we have a Plan B," Momma said. "How many plans do you think we might need?"

"I've gone into Y and Z in the past and still needed more," I admitted.

"Suzanne, thank you for including me in your investigation. I miss our time together," she said as she touched my hand lightly.

I didn't have the heart to tell her that she was my final choice, my last resort. "I've missed you, too," which was the absolute and utter truth. So what if it had taken me some time to get to her to act as my partner in crime?

A few minutes later the front doorbell rang.

Momma looked startled. "Surely he's not here already."

"You'd be surprised. Don't forget, you paid the special delivery bonus," I said as I stood. "Shall I answer the door, or would you like to?"

"I will," she said as she reached for her purse.

"Don't be so eager to pay him right away," I said. "We can use the time you're searching for your 'lost' wallet to interview him."

Momma smiled as she shoved her entire purse under the sofa, barely able to make it fit there. I knew from experience that the bag was heavy, and if it were ever used as a weapon, the results could be quite deadly. "My, aren't you a devious little thing."

"What can I say? I was raised by the best," I said with a grin. "Are you ready for this? It's show time."

"Let us begin, then," she said as she answered the door.

CHAPTER 5

"I'VE GOT YOUR ORDER, MA'AM," Stevie Marks said as Momma opened the door. "That will be forty-seven seventy-five, excluding tip."

I admired the way he'd just reminded her that gratuities were extra. He'd done it boldly, happily, without the least hint of guilt in his voice. I often felt bad about having a tip jar on my counter, and I wouldn't have done that at all if it hadn't been for Emma. Stevie was tall and rail thin, with a mop of brown hair that seemed to be constantly in his eyes. It was no wonder that he was so skinny. If I kept his schedule for a week, I was sure I'd finally lose those last twelve pounds that had been haunting me for years.

I wasn't sure that it would be worth being sleep deprived and run ragged, and besides, Jake liked the way I looked.

"Oh, dear," Momma said, overacting her part. "I seem to have misplaced my wallet."

Stevie seemed nonplussed by the confession. "Tell you what. I'll just set these down on the counter for you while you search for it." He glanced at me and said, "Hey, Ms. Hart. How are you?"

"I'm good, Stevie, despite what happened this morning. Have you heard the news?"

"Are you kidding? Everybody around town is talking about it. I don't know about you, but the body count in our little town is getting kind of scary, isn't it? I'm not sure we even need

Fright Week, but I'm going to take advantage of it. I've got three hundred glow sticks coming in tomorrow, and if I can unload even half of them, I'll make a tidy profit."

"Can't folks buy those elsewhere?" Momma asked, forgetting the reason we had summoned the deliveryman there.

"Sure, if they think about them ahead of time and get them either at one of the stores or online. What I offer is convenience. Never underestimate the laziness of the American consumer," he added with a grin. "I know it hasn't failed me so far."

"Did you happen to see anything this morning yourself when you were delivering newspapers?" I asked him as Momma pretended to search for her wallet.

Stevie frowned upon hearing the question. "That's what the police chief asked me this morning."

"What did you say?" I asked him.

"I told him no," Stevie said with a hint of uncertainty in his voice.

"But now you're thinking differently?" I asked him, basing my question on the timbre in his words.

"I might have seen *something*, but the more I think about it, I'm not sure if it might have just been my imagination supplying something that really wasn't there," he said. "I feel kind of foolish even saying it out loud to you now."

"Please, feel free to tell us. You're among friends here," I said, though I hardly knew him all that well at all. "We won't tell anyone."

After a moment, he shrugged. "I don't see what it could hurt. As I was turning the corner at the clock this morning—I never even looked at the dunking booth, so I couldn't swear if that poor guy was up there or not—I might have seen a long black-and-orange scarf disappear behind Cutnip. Then again, it might have just been a bit of trash floating around in the wind. When I came back through, whatever it might have been was gone."

Cutnip, our local beauty parlor, was located on the other

side of the town clock and near where the dunking booth had been set up. "Did you get any impression at all about who might have been wearing the scarf?" I asked him.

"Like I said, I never even saw the person, if there was even one there. You know what? The more I think about it, the more I'm sure that it was just a piece of a banner or something blowing in the breeze. There are signs all over town promoting Fright Week. That's probably all that it was." Stevie's phone rang, a rather insistent ringtone that sounded a great deal like a UFO landing. "Stevie here. Yes, sir. I'll be right there. I'm just at Mrs. Hart's place, but I'll be leaving in ten seconds. The senior Mrs. Hart. Yes, sir. Okay, thanks." Stevie turned to look at Momma. "Tell you what. I know you're good for it. When you find your wallet, give me a call, and I'll swing back by and pick up the money later."

I nodded to Momma, who magically found her handbag in the next moment. It was a wonder she hadn't had to lift up the couch to remove it. "Eureka. I've got it right here. How did it ever get under there?"

I knew because I'd seen her put it there, but I wasn't about to answer that particular question. After Momma paid him, I noticed Stevie smile at the rather inflated tip she'd presented him.

My mother looked him firmly in the eyes as she said, "Young man, if you should run across any errant memories later or glean any new information about that poor unfortunate man my daughter found, I do hope you'll share it with us immediately."

"You can count on it," Stevie said as he pocketed the cash and headed for the door.

Once he was gone, I asked, "Wow, you are really generous with delivery people, aren't you?"

"I did it for two reasons, Suzanne. One, he will be more

willing in the future to share with us anything he remembers or might learn in the meantime."

"And the second?"

"I admire anyone with an industrious bent," she said with a shrug. "The world needs more folks like that young man, and I aim to encourage him. Now, what do we do with the information we just received?"

"We can't just walk around town asking folks if they might have a black-and-orange scarf tucked away in their closet," I said. "Or can we?" I added after having a thought.

"I can answer that. No, we can't. It sounds rather distinctive, doesn't it?"

"I think so," I said. "And if you were looking for distinctive clothing in April Springs, where would you go?"

"ReNEWed," Momma said, finishing my thought for me.

"Exactly. Maybe, if we're lucky, Gabby sold it to someone recently, and if she did, I'm willing to bet she remembers every last detail about it."

"Then let's go ask her, shall we?" Momma asked.

When we got to Momma's driveway, she recoiled as I opened the passenger door. "Young lady, I'm not going anywhere in that vehicle," she said stiffly.

"Come on. I've seen you ride around town in Phillip's pickup truck, and my Jeep is newer and nicer than that."

"Be that as it may, there are things I will do for my husband that I will not do for you," she said.

"Be a sport, Momma. You might like it."

I didn't think I had a chance of persuading her to ride with me, but to my surprise, after pondering it for a moment, Momma shrugged and got in through the passenger door. "Fine. I suppose I owe it to myself at least once to see why you find this automobile so alluring that when you wrecked one, you immediately went out and bought another exactly like it."

"I didn't exactly wreck it by accident," I said, remembering how harrowing that particular moment had been for me. I'd escaped with my life, both from the impact and the killer, but it was something that I'd never forget. "These are fun to drive. If you'd like, you can take the wheel yourself."

Momma actually blanched a little at the thought. "Thank you, but no. How does this seat belt work?" she asked in frustration.

I grinned as I showed her. "Simple. It's just like every other car you've ever been in."

"I sincerely doubt that," Momma said. Once she was safely belted in, she said, "You do have quite a view in this, don't you?"

"I can even take the doors off if you'd like," I said with a grin. "You can really see everything then. Should I pull over and do it? We can put the top down, too."

"No, I can see just fine as things stand now," Momma said quickly. "Besides, it's much too chilly to be riding around without doors or roofs."

"Suit yourself, but that's when I like it the most," I said. "At least it's not raining."

Momma peered up at the sky. "For now, at any rate. Must you insist on driving so fast, Suzanne? Taking three extra minutes won't impede our investigation that much."

"I'm driving two miles under the speed limit as it is," I said with a grin. "It just feels faster in my Jeep. That's one of the things I love most about it."

"Perhaps I'll walk back home once we're finished with Gabby," she said.

"Suit yourself," I answered with a smile. "I'll be sure to wave to you as I drive by."

Momma clearly wasn't sure how to react for a moment, but

finally, a grin of her own shone through. "I apologize. I've just got a lot on my mind, but there's no reason to take it out on you. I'm sure this is a fine motor vehicle."

"Having trouble at home?" I asked, hoping beyond hope that she didn't answer the question.

"No, it's nothing like that. A business deal I'd been hoping to make fell through at the last moment, and it made me cross. I was all set to buy a particular property, but the seller changed his mind at the last second. I've been hoping that he'll reconsider. His terms are a bit eccentric, but I'll comply with them if I can make this deal happen."

"Surely you own enough property for ten people," I said. "Do you honestly need more?" My momma was our local version of a modern-day land baron, and even I, her only child, had no idea of the exact length and depth of her holdings. "What's one more acre or less in the scheme of things?"

"After a while, it isn't about the land anymore. They are almost like parcels on a Monopoly board. I just enjoy acquiring them and, when the time is right, selling them off."

"Always at a profit though, right?"

She grinned as I pulled up in front of Gabby's shop, which happened to be right beside Donut Hearts. "Nearly always, anyway."

"So, what was so special about this piece?" I asked her.

"It was in Hickory on the Catawba River. I've been watching it for months, and when it finally went on the market, I jumped. Oh, well. I'm sure another piece will come up for sale eventually. Now, let's go see if Gabby can help us, shall we?"

"We shall," I said.

"Hang on one second," I said just before we walked through the door.

"What's wrong, Suzanne? Are you having second thoughts about speaking with Gabby?"

"No, if anything, I want to talk to her now more than ever."

"Why is that?" Momma asked, clearly perplexed by my behavior.

"Have a look at that," I said as I pointed to the display window.

A mannequin was standing there in a little black dress, but that wasn't what had caught my attention.

Wrapped around its neck was a long scarf.

It just happened to be black and orange, just as Stevie had described to us earlier.

The real question was what was it doing in Gabby's front window?

"Gabby, where did you get that scarf on display up front?" I asked as I burst through the door, Momma close on my heels.

"Good afternoon to you, too, Suzanne. Hello, Dot."

"Gabby, it's lovely to see you. How are you?"

"Delightful, thank you for asking," the shop owner said before she turned to me. "Now, what is it you want to know?"

"The scarf in the window. When did it come in? Was it this morning, by any chance?"

Gabby frowned. "Suzanne, there are over three thousand items in this shop. Do you honestly expect me to know when I took in each and every piece? I'd have to have an amazing mind to be able to do that, now wouldn't I?"

"I know you have a system with your notecards, Gabby, so don't try to be coy with me. This is important."

"Why?" Gabby asked, clearly incredulous that a scarf's status could be of any significance to me at all.

"It might be tied to something that happened early this morning," I said, trying to be as vague as I could manage.

"This morning, you say?" she asked. "Tell me more."

Momma stepped up. "Gabrielle, suffice it to say that it matters to us, and we'd like an answer, if you please."

I hadn't heard Gabby's given name used in her presence more than three times in all of the years I'd known her. I was certain that Momma had used it intentionally to show her that we weren't just asking an idle question. What was more, Gabby must have known it, too. "It was tied to my front doorknob this morning when I arrived," she admitted. "I get donations sometimes, but I'm rarely able to use them. They are normally threadbare, soiled, or out of fashion, but being that this is Fright Week, I decided to add it to my dry-cleaning order, and I just received it back not ten minutes ago. It's fetching, given the holiday. Why, would you like to purchase it?"

I was about to refuse when Momma surprised me. "How much are you asking for it, considering you got it for nothing?" Was she dickering now for the sake of haggling on a price, or was there another reason she wanted it?

"It's a steal at twenty-five dollars," Gabby said.

"I'll give you five," Momma said without blinking an eye.

"Why, the dry-cleaning alone cost me more than that," Gabby answered, pretending to be offended by the mere suggestion.

"We both know that you must get a massive discount on your cleaning bill, given the volume of clothes you have laundered, so if it was more than two dollars, I'd be amazed. I'll give you seven," Momma countered.

"I couldn't let it go for anything less than fifteen, and that's taking advantage of me."

"I don't mind a woman making a profit, but let's be reasonable," Momma said. "Nine?"

"Twelve," Gabby said, "and that's my final offer."

Momma studied her for a moment, and then she pulled out

her wallet and produced a ten and two ones. "Sold. It's a pleasure doing business with you."

To my surprise, Gabby smiled right back at her. "I like a woman who knows how to haggle. The pleasure was all mine. Let me get that scarf out of the window for you."

As she left to retrieve it, I asked my mother, "Was there a reason for that purchase, or were you just having a little fun?"

"Gabby claims she doesn't know who donated it, but I wonder," Momma said softly.

"Do you think she's protecting someone?" I asked.

She was about to answer my question when Gabby returned. "Enjoy it in good health," she said as she wrapped it and placed it in a bag for Momma.

"I shall," my mother said.

"Will there be anything else?" Gabby asked.

"Not for the moment," Momma said, and I followed her outside.

"Would you mind telling me what we're going to do with it now that we have it?"

"I'm afraid the explanation is going to have to wait. We need to move quickly right now."

"Why is that?" I asked as Momma opened the bag, discarded the packaging in a nearby trash can, and wrapped the scarf around her neck.

"We need to go to the Boxcar and see if anyone reacts to my new purchase."

"That's a nice scarf you've got there, Dot," Trish said to Momma the moment we walked into the converted train boxcar that now was my favorite spot to eat out in April Springs. "It's really festive, isn't it?"

"I just bought it at ReNEWed," Momma said proudly. "Why would anyone give this up at the beginning of Fright Week?"

"Beats me," Trish said as she touched it lightly. "The behavior of the common man continually baffles me."

"Or common woman," I added.

"I'd love to get its history," Momma continued. "Have you ever seen it before, Trish? I'm dying to meet the last owner."

"I can't say that it looks all that familiar to me," Trish conceded.

Momma looked disappointed, but I knew how many dead ends and wastes of time investigations tended to have. "Thanks, Trish," I said. "If you think of anybody, let us know."

The grill owner lowered her voice and moved closer toward us, though no one else was anywhere near the cash register up front at the moment. "Is this about the man you found this morning, Suzanne?"

"It might be," I conceded. It was better to get Trish as an ally right up front than to mislead her and have to ask for forgiveness later.

"*He* wasn't wearing it, was he?" she asked in a surprised voice as she studied it again. "I suppose a man might choose to wear that out in public, but he'd have to be braver than most of the men I know."

"No, he wasn't wearing it, but whoever donated it to Gabby might have seen something at the crime scene without even realizing it," I said.

Momma looked surprised by my explanation, but I doubted that Trish could tell. I'd learned long ago that it was easier to get information about a potential witness than it was a possible killer. Folks were more apt to talk when it didn't directly involve whatever bad guy we were looking for at the time. "Doesn't Gabby know who she bought it from?" she asked.

"She claims that somebody left it tied to her doorknob this morning, so she had it cleaned and put on sale by the time we got there ten minutes ago," I said.

"So *you* bought it? What makes you think that it might be tied to a witness?" Trish asked, keen to get the inside scoop on our investigation.

I knew that I could trust her, but there were a great many folks in the diner at the moment, and I wasn't at all sure they couldn't overhear our conversation, given the propensity of our little town towards gossip. "Suffice it to say that someone spotted it this morning, but they couldn't see who might have been wearing it," I said, barely above a whisper now.

"Got it. So, it *could* have belonged to the killer. I have a question, if that's the case. If Stevie saw someone wearing that this morning, why would someone ditch it at Gabby's? Why not stick it in the bottom of the closet, or better yet, put it in a trash bag and throw it into the nearest dumpster?"

I knew that something had been bothering me about the scarf's sudden appearance in Gabby's front window, and Trish had just put her finger on it. "That's exactly what we want to find out," I said.

Momma was frowning yet again, but I was making it up as we went along now. There were no neatly laid out scripts in my investigations. I was a firm believer in going with the flow and seeing what might turn up.

"Okay, but don't go telling everyone the same thing you told me. It wouldn't be fair to Stevie to put him on the spot like that."

I was surprised for a moment by her accurately naming our source, and I was about to deny it when Momma beat me to it.

"You must understand that we can't confirm or deny any potential witness we may have spoken with," she said.

"You don't have to," Trish said with a grin. "Who else would be out at that time of morning besides you, Suzanne? I'm assuming you didn't spot the scarf yourself." I was about to protest, however feebly, when Trish put her finger to her lips and added, "You know you don't have to worry about me. Mum's the word."

I was about to answer when I scanned the room and found someone in particular trying very hard not to stare at Momma's scarf and failing miserably at it. It was Jenny Preston, the woman who owned For The Birds, and when we made eye contact, she practically leapt up from her table, her meal still half eaten, and pushed her way past us with nary a word.

Momma and Trish had missed the exchange, but I wasn't about to let it go. I tapped Momma's arm as I pivoted and headed for the door myself.

"Was it something I said?" Trish asked.

"We'll be back," I said.

Momma, to my great relief, didn't ask me a single question about my abrupt behavior.

She simply followed my lead.

CHAPTER 6

"J ENNY! WAIT UP!"

"I'm sorry. I didn't see you," Jenny Preston said as she finally slowed enough for us to catch up with her. "I apologize, but I can't really talk at the moment. I need to get back to the store."

"That's fine. We'll walk with you," I said as I tried to match her pace. Momma found a way to keep up with her more easily than I did, which peeved me a little, since her legs were quite a bit shorter than mine.

"Suit yourself," Jenny said as she hurried down the block toward her shop, one that catered to bird lovers by offering all kinds of goodies from sunflower seed blends to ornately crafted feeders to more varieties of suet blends than I'd ever thought possible. I wasn't sure how she stayed afloat in our small town, but she seemed to be doing just fine.

"Tell me what made you react to Momma's scarf back at the Boxcar Grill," I said.

Jenny hesitated for a few moments before answering, but she took too long to respond to be credible in her denial. "I'm certain I don't know what you're talking about."

"There's no use denying it. I saw your face the moment you saw it wrapped around her neck," I said. "So I'll ask you again. Why the intense reaction?"

"I'm sure it was just your imagination," Jenny answered, trying her best to sound casual and utterly failing.

"And I'm just as certain that it wasn't," I said firmly.

We were at her shop now, and Jenny looked almost relieved to be there. "As I said before, I'm really sorry, but I really can't talk. I have inventory to do."

"In late October?" I asked her.

"We run on a different fiscal calendar than most folks do," she said after a few moments.

I didn't believe her for a second. "But you're still open for business, right? The reason I ask is that I see at least three people inside shopping right now, and Margaret is waiting on them. How long has she been working for you, by the way?"

"A while now," Jenny said.

"What about the shoppers still inside?" I pressed.

"We'll just have to ask them to leave, since we're about to close for the day," she said, nearly choking on her words.

"Then Momma and I will come in and shop until you do. That will give us a chance to chat about the scarf a little more. You don't mind if anyone overhears us, do you?"

I could tell in an instant that Jenny would mind that very much, but she couldn't exactly deny us entry without throwing her legitimate customers out at the same time. "Fine. I'll tell you. I don't know *why* I reacted the way I did. I suppose it was because I never expected to see it on *your* neck, Dot," she said as she looked at Momma. "When I saw it at ReNEWed, I thought it would make a perfect gift for a friend of mine, but when I tried to buy it, I was told that it wasn't for sale."

That didn't sound right. Gabby often boasted that she'd sell the entire building if the price was right. "Who told you that it wasn't available for purchase?" I asked her.

"Gabby said so herself. It was in one of the bins, but when I tried to buy it, she told me that I couldn't, because she was keeping it for herself. Gabby made some flimsy excuse that it had gotten out onto the sales floor by accident, and that was that. Or so I thought."

"When exactly did this happen?" I asked. Had Jenny approached Gabby just before *we'd* arrived? If so, why did the shopkeeper refuse to sell it to her but then offer it to us a little later? Things were just not adding up, and in my world, I preferred things to make sense. Honestly, who didn't?

"It was yesterday afternoon, just as she was beginning to close for the day," Jenny said.

"That's impossible," Momma blurted out. "Are you sure you aren't mistaken?"

"Dot, I know today from yesterday. The reason I kept staring at you at the Boxcar was because I really wanted that scarf to give as a gift, and when I saw that Gabby had sold it to you instead, it just got under my skin."

"Tell you what, when this is all over, I'll sell it to you myself," Momma said. "In fact, it will be a gift from me to you."

"Thanks, but I don't honestly want it under those conditions. It's a bit tainted for me. Now I really do have to get back to work."

"Go on, and have a good inventory," I said.

Jenny stumbled for a moment as she struggled for a reply, and I was happy to see that she was so unused to lying that she could barely bring herself to do it competently.

"What is going on, Suzanne?" Momma asked me a moment later. "This doesn't make sense. First Trish points out that there is no reason for that scarf to show up at ReNEWed this morning, and then Jenny tells us that Gabby had it yesterday, not this morning as she reported to us, and what is more, she refused to sell it to Jenny so she could keep it for herself. Was she the one Stevie spotted this morning? I find it hard to believe, but we have to consider it a possibility. The truth is that I don't understand any of it."

"Neither do I," I said. Could Gabby have had something to do with the stranger's demise, if it had indeed been murder? I could hardly imagine her just out for a late-night stroll. There were questions that demanded answers, and only the owner of ReNEWed could provide them. "That's why we're marching straight back to Gabby's shop and talking to her again. We're not leaving until we get answers, either."

"Agreed," Momma said.

We were to be thwarted in our goal, though.

When we got back to ReNEWed, though we'd only been gone from there for less than half an hour, the CLOSED sign was in the window, and the front door was locked.

Apparently it wasn't going to be as easy to talk to Gabby as I'd hoped.

"I've got to say that was odd behavior earlier, even from the pair of you," Trish said when we walked back into the Boxcar. "You both took off out of here as though your hair was on fire. What was the hurry?"

"I wanted to check something out while it was still fresh in my mind," I said, which wasn't a complete lie.

"What did Jenny have to say about the scarf?" Trish asked with that wicked grin of hers.

"What are you talking about?" I asked, feigning ignorance.

It just made Trish's grin even broader. "Seriously, Suzanne? You're going to try to play dumb with *me*?"

"I just wish it was playing," I said. "Okay, I did want to speak with Jenny. She spotted Momma's scarf the moment we walked in, and she couldn't take her eyes off of it the entire time."

"Was she your mystery witness this morning? It wasn't

Stevie?" Trish asked eagerly. She really did yearn to be involved in one of my investigations, but the timing hadn't been right for us, at least not at that point. Who knew what the future might hold?

"No, but she told us something intriguing," I admitted. I was about to say that I couldn't talk about it when Momma said, "Suzanne, that table over there is free. Let's have a late lunch, shall we?"

"Sure. Why not?" I asked, frowning at her odd interruption.

Trish put a hand on my arm before I could go, though. "I'm dying to know. What did Jenny tell you?"

At that moment, Cal Jeffries approached the cash register with his bill and a ten in his hand. I could tell Trish wanted to blow him off, but she wasn't about to let money she'd earned walk through the door. "We'll catch up on the rest of it later."

"That's really all there is to it for now," I said.

"Should I believe you?" Trish asked.

"Hey, Trish, I can't wait forever," Cal said. "Should we just settle this up later?"

"No, I'm coming," she said, her business taking precedence over her curiosity, at least for the moment.

As we sat down at the free table, Momma said, "You can't tell her *everything* we're doing and thinking, Suzanne. It's not appropriate."

"Momma, I trust Trish with my life, but I wasn't going to tell her about Gabby, especially not before we had a chance to speak with her again ourselves," I explained.

"Oh. Sorry. I may have jumped the gun." It was an outright apology, something I wasn't accustomed to getting from my mother.

"No worries," I said, letting it slide. I appreciated the gesture, and what was more, I knew that if I made a fuss about it, it would be a long time before she did it again. "After we eat, we can check back on ReNEWed and see if Gabby has returned."

"And if she hasn't, we can always just hunt her down," Momma said.

"I'm not sure I like the word 'hunt' in that context," I countered. "At the moment, we don't have any reason to suspect her of committing murder."

"I'm not at all certain that we should be so willing to discount the prospect that it might be true," Momma said.

"Do you honestly think that it was *Gabby* Stevie saw this morning leaving the scene?" I asked her softly.

"We must consider the *possibility* that it's true; that's all that I'm saying. Suzanne, I know you are fond of her, but we must put that aside if we're going to do a proper job of this. In all of my years, I've learned that I must subjugate my feelings and judge things based on facts, not suppositions."

"That's commendable of you," I said as Trish approached. "I'm just not sure I can do that."

"I admit that it's difficult for me as well at times," Momma said with the hint of a smile. "Still, it's nice to have lofty goals, isn't it?"

"I suppose so, as long as they don't get in the way of you living your life," I replied.

When Trish reached us, I saw that she was carrying two glasses of sweet tea, though we hadn't ordered anything yet.

"I thought you two looked thirsty," she said as she placed them in front of us.

"We are," I said with a smile after I took my first sip of the deliciously sweet concoction. "Are we hungry, too?"

Trish pretended to study us, each in our turn, before answering. "I'd say two manager's specials would be perfect."

"That sounds good to me," I said.

Momma wasn't quite so eager to accept her recommendation, though. "What exactly *is* the special today?"

"We're having turkey, stuffing, mashed potatoes, and cranberry sauce," she said. "I know Halloween is approaching, but I asked the girls to make us a Thanksgiving treat early. How does that sound to you?"

"Delightful," Momma said.

"Are the potatoes sculpted into the shape of a ghost?" I asked Trish.

"I suppose we can do it if that's the way you'd like them," she said. "Why would you want that, though?"

"I just figured George and Cassandra would be asking you to pump up Fright Week with your menu," I said.

"I agreed to go along with the theme, but I'm not starting until tomorrow. Don't tell me they got to you, too."

I grinned. "Actually, Emma decided we needed to go all out before they could manage to even ask. We're selling donut-hole eyeballs and donuts with cobwebs all over them, and that's just the start."

"Apparently everybody in town is getting on board," Trish allowed. "That Cassandra is a force to be reckoned with, isn't she?"

"So then, what will be on the menu tomorrow?" Momma asked.

"We're featuring ghost soup, which is really just our potato soup without the carrots, and finger sandwiches, cut out in the shapes of actual fingers."

"That sounds difficult to do," I said.

"You'd think so, but it's amazing the types of cutters you can find online these days."

"You don't have to tell me," I said. "We're using several different ones at the shop ourselves."

Trish was summoned up front to collect the money on another tab, so she left us to see to business. "I'll have your food out to you in a second."

After she was gone to take care of business, Momma asked me softly, "Is it my imagination, or is Trish overly interested in what we're up to?"

"It's hard to judge. If I had to guess, I'd say it's her normal amount of inquisitiveness. Why, do you think it's odd?"

"I've never known her to be so aggressive trying to learn what you were doing in the past, but maybe it's just me," Momma said.

I gave it some thought, and then I said, "You know something? I think you might be right. She seems to want to know more than usual. Do you think that means she knows more than she's letting on about the dead stranger?"

"I know how fond you are of her. I am, too. I'm just pointing out that it might not be a bad idea to hold a few things back from her until we know the lay of the land."

I patted my mother's hand, a gesture that conveyed a great deal of love with it. "That's good advice, Momma. Thank you."

"You don't *really* think she's involved, do you?" Momma asked me. "What I was saying earlier was just sheer speculation."

"I don't know, but that's kind of the point, isn't it? I'll try to be a little more circumspect in the future."

As I said it, Trish suddenly appeared, carrying two plates. "Sorry about the wait."

"It's amazing how fast you are," Momma said.

"Everything's already been made in back. We just plate it and serve it. I hope you enjoy your meals, ladies."

As promised, the plate also sported a dollop of cranberry sauce as well. "Goodie. Thanksgiving dessert," I said.

"We didn't make pumpkin pie. I'm sorry," Trish said.

"I was talking about the cranberry sauce," I said as I poked it with my fork and grinned.

"Gotcha. I was hoping to join you so we could chat more, but things are surprisingly busy for this time of day."

Momma glanced at me with arched eyebrows, but Trish couldn't see it from her vantage point. "Next time for sure," I said.

After she was gone, Momma said, "Curiouser and curiouser."

"Don't start quoting Lewis Carroll to me," I said, "no matter how much I agree with the sentiment."

I took a bite of turkey and smiled. I knew that after the coming holidays I'd be thoroughly tired of eating it, but at the moment, it served as a nice change of pace from meatloaf and hamburgers. One thing was certain. Without power and water at my cottage, I wouldn't be making anything except reservations for the next several days. Staying with Momma wasn't about to improve the hope of me making a home-cooked meal, either. After all, it was my mother's kitchen, and I was allowed in only on a case-by-case basis. Then again, I could just be a complete freeloader and let her cook for all of us. Goodness knew she enjoyed it. Still, there was something about being a grownup that made me bristle at the thought of my mother feeding me on a daily basis again.

As I scooped up a bite of mashed potato, I heard someone from a nearby table say, "It's not right holding this spooky celebration when a man died not thirty feet from where we're sitting."

"The mayor's lost all sense of judgment," an older woman answered. "What is he thinking?"

"I'm not sure that he's thinking at all," the man replied. "That woman has cast some kind of spell over him. He hasn't been himself since she showed up."

I was about to speak up in George's defense, despite a niggling bit of me agreeing with them, when someone did it for me. Trish must have heard them chatting too as she'd been offering refills of sweet tea. I hadn't even noticed her standing there, but when she started talking loudly, there was no mistaking her. "Robert, you and Cynthia Lynn should know that I won't have treason spoken at my restaurant."

"Treason? We didn't say anything bad about the country," Robert protested.

"Maybe not directly, but you were slamming my mayor, who also happens to be my friend. I believe in free speech as much as the next gal, but I also believe in my right to refuse to serve anyone I please, for whatever reason I choose."

The overt threat hung in the air between them for a moment before Cynthia Lynn spoke softly. "We didn't mean anything by it, Trish. George is a good man."

"You'd better believe he is," Trish said, and then she smiled as she added, "Can I top off your sweet teas?"

"Please," Robert said softly.

Trish did as she'd promised, and she even managed a smile for the pair before she left them. "I'll have your bills ready for you in a second."

As Trish stopped at our table to top our own glasses off before she walked back up front, I said, "Thanks. I was about to say something myself."

In a soft voice, Trish said, "They're not completely wrong though, are they? You should have a talk with George."

"Do you think he'd actually listen to me?" I asked her.

"I'm sorry. I was talking to your mother," Trish said, looking directly at Momma now.

"Me? What makes you think the mayor would listen to me?"

"Come on, Dot, this is no time to be modest. Your voice carries a lot of weight around here."

"And what exactly am I supposed to say, Patricia?" Momma asked sternly, using my friend's full given name.

Trish suddenly blushed, and I wanted to leap to her defense, but before I could, she said, "You're right. I just hate to see him making a fool of himself, even if he is doing it because he's in love."

"How do you believe he is making a fool of himself?" Momma asked, not letting up on her.

"Sometimes I wonder if Cassandra has suddenly become his co-mayor," she said, voicing aloud what I'd been wondering myself. "He's a dear friend, but that doesn't mean he gets a free pass when it comes to the good of April Springs."

"Then if you feel so strongly about it, you should speak with him yourself," Momma said, finally softening up a bit. "I believe he's still doing what's best for our town. April Springs has made a rather large financial commitment to Fright Week, and to cancel it now would be ruinous for the budget."

"There are more things in life than money, Momma," I said.

"Yes, I'm well aware of that fact, Suzanne. My point is that shutting the festivities down at this time won't help that unfortunate man."

Trish looked at me, and all I could do was shrug. "Thanks anyway," Trish said as she made her way back to the front to prepare Cynthia Lynn and Robert's bills.

"You were kind of tough on her just then, weren't you?" I asked Momma after swallowing another bite of food.

"Perhaps. I'm just growing weary of being asked to champion every unpopular opinion just because I supposedly have clout in this town." In a softer voice, she added, "Besides, if Fright Week were to be cancelled, we might never find out what happened to the moon-faced man."

"I wish you'd stop calling him that," I said, shivering a little at the sound of the temporary moniker we'd given the dead man.

"When I know his proper name, I shall use it, but in the interim, we have to call him something."

My meal was nearly finished, but the truth was that my appetite was gone, anyway. Momma had eaten less than half her meal, but that was standard operating procedure for her. There was a reason I was fifteen pounds overweight and she still weighed what she did in high school.

Trish clearly wanted to talk more when we approached the register, but three other diners decided to leave just after we did, and there was quite a line vying for her attention.

"Keep me posted," was all she could manage as we started to walk out.

"We'll do our best," I said, not sure that was true at all. I hated lying to my friend, but I didn't feel as though I had any choice, especially if Trish might be tied up with the man who'd so recently passed away.

The moon-faced man, as Momma had said.

I hoped Chief Grant discovered his name, and soon.

A cause of death would be even nicer.

If he'd died from something natural, Momma and I could quit instantly, but until we knew what had really happened to him, we had no choice but to move forward.

And that meant tracking Gabby Williams down and finding out the real story behind that Halloween-colored scarf.

CHAPTER 7

"HOW CAN SHE JUST DISAPPEAR like that?" Momma asked after we spent a frustrating hour trying to find Gabby Williams. We'd checked ReNEWed again, her place, and even a few of her friends, including Margaret.

If anyone knew where she was, they weren't sharing the news with us.

"You'd be surprised how easy it is. She might have even left town to avoid talking to us," I said as we sat in front of Donut Hearts in dejection.

"Suzanne, don't be overly dramatic."

"Momma, you'd be amazed if you knew the number of people who go out of their way to avoid me when I'm working on an investigation."

"Don't you ever get disheartened by it all?" my mother asked gently.

"I try not to take it personally," I explained.

"And are you successful in achieving that goal?"

"I'll let you know if it ever happens," I answered her with a grin.

"So what do we do now, just give up?" Momma said, clearly unhappy about the sad state of our investigation.

"If we do that, we might as well throw in the towel and quit altogether," I said.

"I honestly don't know what else we *can* do," she said. "We've

70

spoken to everyone we think might have known the moon-faced man, and now Gabby is on the run."

"Maybe her taking off is just a coincidence," I said, though I rarely believed in them. Still, sometimes they happened despite my lack of willingness to embrace happenstance.

"How can you possibly explain that?"

"You know Gabby. She's been known to close her shop on the slightest whim. If that's not it, she could have a sick relative, she might have decided at the last minute to take a trip, or she could have left town to get away from the Fright Week activities," I said. "The mayor and Cassandra told me that she's about the only shopkeeper in town who hasn't embraced the festival."

"I still think we should ask Van Rayburn about her," Momma said. "Last week I saw them out in the park canoodling like a pair of teenagers."

"We could try, but I heard through the grapevine that she and Van were taking a break," I said. I'd overheard the gossip in my donut shop a few days before, but I'd been reluctant to approach Gabby to see if it was actually true.

"What can it hurt to ask him, Suzanne?" Momma asked as she got out her cell phone and made the call. After a minute, she frowned as she ended it. "It went straight to voicemail, and then there was a message that said he'd be unavailable for the next few days. For all we know, they could be off together somewhere reconciling."

"I suppose anything is possible. We also have to consider the possibility that Jenny was lying to us earlier."

"Why on earth would she do that?" Momma asked me.

"What if she knows more than she claims to about the man I found this morning?" I was doing my best not to call him the moon-faced man, but it was hard not to, given the fact that we didn't have a name for him yet.

"If she lied to us about the scarf, wouldn't Gabby be able to easily refute it the moment we asked her?" Momma asked me.

"You'd be surprised how some people will tell a lie without thinking it through completely," I assured her. "I've caught more than one bad guy in the past because of it."

"Then we need to speak with Jenny again and press her a little harder," Momma said with clear and firm resolve.

Before she could get out of the Jeep though, I put a hand on her arm. "I've got a better idea. Let's wait until we speak with Gabby again first. If we confront Jenny and call her a liar, which is what more questioning about the scarf would be at this point, we're not only liable to lose a potential witness but a friend as well."

"I wish we had a way of compelling her to talk to us," my mother said, quite out of character for her. It was obvious that she was getting frustrated with the situation, but then again, why wouldn't she be? She was a woman of action if there ever was one, and the way we had to investigate clearly wasn't working for her.

"That's the police's bailiwick," I said. "We have to question folks using only cleverness and guile."

"It's harder than it looks, isn't it?" Momma asked.

"It can be," I admitted.

"So, if we can't make answering our questions compulsory, and we are missing the one person we need to speak with before we do anything else, what is there left for us to do?"

"We could always search for clues," I said.

"I'm all for that course of action, but where do we even start?"

I thought about it for a few moments, and then I said, "Let's leave the Jeep right here and start walking toward the clock. Who knows? Maybe we'll get lucky and find something."

"Haven't the police already searched the immediate area?" Momma asked me a little petulantly. Her frustration was coming through clearly.

"I'm sure they've searched some of it, but what else do we have to do at the moment? The men are no doubt busy destroying the cottage, so we can't exactly count on them to entertain us."

"Very well, then. Let's take a walk and see what we can see," Momma said.

We got out of the Jeep, locked it up, and started walking toward the town clock where I'd found the stranger's body just a handful of hours earlier.

"This is absolutely useless, Suzanne," Momma said after we'd covered both sides of Springs Drive all the way to the town clock and back again without seeing a single thing of significance. I'd even ducked around the side and the back of Cutnip to see if I could spot something the mysterious scarfed person might have dropped, but nothing unusual or noteworthy caught my eye. We were finally back to where we'd started, beside the Jeep, which was still parked in front of Donut Hearts. It looked as though it belonged there to me.

Momma sighed, and then she asked, "We aren't going to find a thing, but even if we do, how do we know if it is significant or not? A gum wrapper might be able to yield a dozen clues, but we'd have no way of knowing it."

"We're just amateurs, so we can't do forensic analysis," I admitted, "but most clues are a little more overt than that. I've found all kinds of things in the past, just because I took the time to look."

"I thought that was what the police were for," Momma said.

"Hey, even the best cop needs a hand sometimes. I helped your husband occasionally, mine more than once, and even the current police chief a time or two. There's nothing wrong with adding another set of eyes and, in this case, two to the case. So what if we didn't find anything? At least we had a nice walk in perfect weather."

"There is always that," Momma said. "What should we do now? I don't know about you, but I'm curious as to whether our men took my conditions to heart. Aren't you?"

"I've spent much too much of my time this afternoon trying *not* to think about that," I said. "Of course I want to know." I glanced across the park toward the cottage and spied a pale teenaged girl sitting on a bench wearing short shorts despite the cool weather, though she did have on an oversized letter jacket, presumably on loan from her boyfriend. She didn't notice us at all. How could she, being as obsessed with her cell phone as she was?

"Let's drive over there and find out," Momma said.

"I have a better idea. Let's walk. If they don't know we're coming, they won't realize that we're there before it is too late to hide their current transgressions."

"My, don't you have a devious mind," Momma said with a smile.

"The apple doesn't fall far from the tree, you know," I answered with a grin of my own.

"I certainly hope not," she said.

We passed the teenager, who was still oblivious to our presence, though I was close enough to reach out and knock the phone right out of her hand if I had a mind to. I would never do it, but it did strike me that a young woman probably not more than fifteen or sixteen and alone in the park was so completely enamored with her electronic world that she wasn't aware of anything going on in the real world around her. I wanted to warn her that she should be more vigilant, that the world could be a cruel and dangerous place, but I knew that most likely all I would get in return was an eye roll at best, and the possibility of much worse. I still considered saying something to her when

I noticed a child's plastic jack o'lantern pumpkin in the bushes just behind her.

"Excuse me, is that yours?" I asked her, standing in a way that my shadow blocked the sun from her.

"What's that?" she asked, refusing even to look up and make eye contact.

"Is that your plastic pumpkin over there?" I asked again.

She didn't even glance at it, or us, for that matter. "No. It's all yours."

As she said it, Momma smiled, but there wasn't a great deal of warmth in it. "You are Lucy Danvers, aren't you?"

That caught her off guard, and she finally looked up from her cell phone. She had short brown hair, clear blue eyes, and shiny braces on her teeth. "How do you know my name?"

"I'm great friends with your grandmother," Momma said softly. "How is she doing, dear?"

"Better," Lucy said as a whisper of a forlorn smile slowly crept onto her face. "The chemo's working. At least that's what they say, because she still looks rough to me. If she's getting better, why are they putting her back into the hospital? I keep checking my phone waiting for news about her, but so far, I haven't heard a thing."

So that explained her obsession with her cell phone. I suddenly felt bad about judging her so harshly earlier.

Momma reached out and patted the girl's shoulder, and I thought for an instant that it was a dangerous move, but the girl's smile suddenly looked as though it were about to break into a thousand tears. "There, there, my dear. Your grandmother is a tough old bird. Don't count her out just yet."

"Thanks," Lucy said as she stood, and to my shock and surprise, the teenager hugged my mother fiercely. "I needed to hear that. I've been sitting here for what feels like hours lost in my own nightmares. I keep expecting to get a call that she's gone. That's why I keep staring at my phone. Sorry if I was rude before."

"You owe us no apologies. Shouldn't you be with your father, though?" Momma asked her. "We'd be glad to drive you to the hospital."

Lucy shook her head. "Thanks, but Dad is putting on a brave face, and I just can't take it anymore. I had to get out of there before I snapped."

Momma took the girl's free hand in hers. "He needs you, my dear. I know it's not fair, but you must be strong for him and your grandmother, Lucy. Can you do that?"

The teenager pondered the question for a moment before nodding. "I can do it if I have to."

Momma pulled out a business card from her purse. "Here is my number. If you need someone to talk to, day or night, call me."

"I will. Thanks." A few tears trickled down her cheeks, but she didn't even seem to notice them. "You're right. I'd better go."

"Be strong, Lucy."

"Thanks. I'll try."

"I'm sure you'll do marvelously."

After the teenaged girl was gone, I turned to my mother in amazement. "How did you do that?"

"Do what, Suzanne?"

"When we saw her sitting there engrossed in her phone, I assumed she was just another sullen teenager, but you not only looked hard enough to really see her, but you did your best to help her in a tough time."

"It was nothing. Anyone else would have done the same," Momma said, clearly a little embarrassed by my overt admiration.

"I wish that were true with all my heart, but you don't know how wrong you are," I said.

"What did you ask her about when you first approached her?" Momma asked me, clearly trying to change the subject. "I missed it."

"I was talking about this," I said as I pushed aside some leaves and retrieved a plastic pumpkin with black eyes, a nose, and a set of crooked teeth.

"It's clearly someone's discard from the festival," Momma said. "Throw it away, Suzanne. It's just trash."

The funny thing was that it didn't feel like trash to me, and it certainly wasn't empty. A man's light jacket was folded up inside, and as I pulled it out, a wallet fell out onto the ground.

"That's odd," Momma said.

"I'm going to open it to see who it belongs to," I said as I leaned down and picked it up.

"Shouldn't you just turn it in to the police, Suzanne?"

"That's probably exactly what I should do," I said with a smile, "but I'm going to have a peek myself first."

Before she could stop me, I flipped the wallet open.

That was when I found the moon-faced man staring back at me from his driver's license photo.

CHAPTER 8

"**S**UZANNE, YOU SHOULDN'T TOUCH ANYTHING in that," Momma said as I took the edge of my T-shirt and pulled out the driver's license so I could get a better look.

After scanning it and then taking a photo of it with my cell phone, I put it back where I'd found it, and as I took more pictures, I said, "I'm not messing up any fingerprints, and we have a right to take a few photos before we call the police chief."

The wallet was nearly empty of any other identifying items or marks, and there was just nine dollars clearly visible inside, along with a folded twenty tucked behind the "secret" section that everyone knew about. I took photos of the cash as well, and then I studied the driver's license again. "His name was Carson Winfield," I said as I read it off. "It says here that he's from Montana. What in the world was he doing in North Carolina?"

"I haven't the slightest idea," Momma said as she looked furtively around. "Suzanne, will you please call the police *now?*"

"Okay, I'll call them," I said as I tucked the wallet back into the jacket and then returned it to the plastic pumpkin. I'd already touched a few of the items before I'd realized their significance, but I knew that the police had my fingerprints on file. It was perfectly natural to assume that I'd check a lost wallet to see who it belonged to. At least that was what I was going to try to sell to the police chief.

"Chief, it's Suzanne Hart."

"Suzanne, I still don't have a cause of death for the man you found this morning. Shoot, I don't even have an ID on him yet."

"His name was Carson Winfield, and he was last known to be living in Montana," I said.

There was a moment's pause before the chief responded. "And how exactly do you know that?"

"Momma and I were walking through the park to surprise Jake and Phillip at the cottage. We spotted a plastic Halloween jack o'lantern in the bushes on the way there. I thought it might be trash, but when I picked it up, I saw that there was a man's jacket inside. When I tried to pull it out to see who it belonged to, a wallet fell on the ground, so naturally I wanted to see who it belonged to so I could return it to them."

"Naturally," Chief Grant said. "I'm guessing that's your way of telling me that your fingerprints are all over it."

"How else could I see who the owner was?" I asked. I saw that Momma was looking at me with a slight hint of disapproval, but I hadn't lied at any point in my conversation to the police chief, at least not so far. Sure, I may have left a few things out, and the things I had told him may have been skewed in my favor, but I hadn't lied.

"Fine," he said with a grumble, accepting my story, at least for the moment. "Don't touch anything else, okay?"

"We'll be here waiting for you. You can't miss us."

He didn't even dignify that with a response, since the park was so small that the moment he entered it, he'd clearly see us.

After I hung up, I said, "No worries, Momma. He's on his way."

"You weren't exactly forthright with him just now, were you?" my mother asked me sternly.

"How do you mean? *Everything* I told him was the truth."

"Perhaps, but you neglected to mention that we were actively searching for a clue as to the man's identity when we found the jack o'lantern."

"Does it really matter what our motivation was?" I asked her. "We found a lost or discarded wallet in the park, and we called the police. It's exactly what any good citizen would do under the same circumstances."

"Are you telling me that they'd take those photographs as well? Suzanne, are you honestly trying to convince me of that, or yourself?"

"Momma, we have one foot in a bucket every time we try to investigate something. If there's a chance we can learn something and we let it pass us by, who are we helping? Besides, who gets hurt by what we did? The police will have every bit of evidence we found. We're not withholding anything." I'd made it a point to continually use "we" instead of "I." I wanted Momma to realize that we were a team in this investigation, and she was just as much a part of it as I was.

"I can see your point when you put it that way," Momma said reluctantly as Chief Grant spotted us and walked over to join us. If Momma's husband had been investigating the case when he was chief, he would have probably come ripping up Springs Avenue in his squad car, his siren screaming and his lights flashing. Chief Grant favored a more low-key approach, something I was most grateful for.

I noticed that the chief was already wearing latex gloves. As he reached for the jack o'lantern, he said, "Hello, ladies. Thanks for calling me. Where exactly did you find this?"

"It was over there under those bushes, and some leaves had been kicked up around it to try to hide it," I explained.

"And you just happened to spot it on your walk home?" he asked skeptically.

"It may have been partially hidden by debris, but it is bright orange, after all," I said. I didn't see any reason to bring Lucy into it, and I was glad that Momma didn't volunteer the young teen's name, either. She had enough on her plate at the moment without being questioned by the police. Besides, she hadn't seen us when we'd been standing right in front of her, so I doubted that she'd be able to help the investigation at all.

The chief took the jacket out carefully, found the wallet immediately, but instead of opening it, he set it aside. Only after he'd done a thorough examination of all of the pockets of the jacket did he fold it back up and replace it where it had been. Then and only then did he take out the wallet and study it. After searching the contents thoroughly, he looked at me again. "Tell me again. This is exactly the way you found it, right?"

"Right," I said. I knew what he was so delicately asking me. The question was fair enough, so I had no problem answering truthfully. If he asked me if I'd taken any photos of what we'd found, I wasn't sure I would have been quite so forthright with the truth.

The chief looked at my mother for confirmation, and after she nodded in agreement, he sighed a little. "Okay. I'll take it from here. Thanks for calling."

"You're welcome," I said. "Will you do me one favor?" I asked as Momma and I started to walk toward the cottage.

"I will if I can," the chief said.

"When you find out the cause of death, would you call me and let me know?" I asked.

"Is that what this is about? Are you two digging into this after all? Ladies, we don't even know if foul play was involved yet."

"Not officially, but what's your gut telling you?" I asked him.

"My gut doesn't play any role in this," he answered curtly.

"We both know better than that, Chief," I said. "If Carson Winfield's death turns out to be natural causes, which I sincerely doubt, then why did he hide his wallet and his jacket all the way over here? My guess is that he was meeting someone, and he was being careful about it."

"Any idea who that might have been?" he asked me.

Momma looked as though she wanted to say something, but I beat her to it. "Like you always tell me, it's too early in the investigation to have many answers yet. We're still trying to figure out what the right questions are we should be asking and who we should be talking to."

"Join the club," he said as another officer arrived, this one carrying video and still-picture equipment.

"You'll call me with news?" I asked him again.

"When I find anything out, and when and if I get the time. That's the best you're going to get out of me. Have a good evening, ladies."

"You, too," I said.

The police chief paused for a moment and sighed before he spoke. "Grace is out of town, but it's probably just as well, since I'm not going to have any free time for her anyway. The truth is that I'll most likely be in my office half the night, and it's already been a long day."

"Sorry about that," I said.

"Hey, it's not your fault," Chief Grant said, and then he promptly dismissed us and started instructing his underling on exactly what he wanted.

As we walked to the cottage, Momma asked, "We're really no closer to uncovering the truth than we were before we found that pumpkin, are we?"

"I don't know if I'd say that."

"I will concede the fact that we have the man's name and his tenuous financial status if his wallet is any indication, but we still don't know why he was here in the first place."

"I'm willing to bet that it wasn't to play tourist," I said.

"The fact that he hid his wallet before he met someone tells us volumes. He anticipated that there might be trouble, and he took precautions. That tells us a great deal. The more we learn, the more I'm willing to bet that he was murdered, and I'm not waiting on the coroner to confirm it."

"What should we do, then?" Momma asked.

"At the moment? I don't have a clue. We need to find Gabby, and we need more information in general. Unfortunately, after we do an Internet search on the man's name, there won't be much we can do." I pulled out my phone and did a quick check on Carson Winfield from Montana. There were no results. It didn't surprise me all that much. A great many folks seem to leave little or no electronic footprints in the web. To dig deeper would take more resources than we had at our disposal. As I put my phone away, I said, "No luck there. Come on, let's go see what the men have been up to."

"How can you just drop it like that?" Momma asked as we walked the final few steps to the cottage.

"What choice do we have? Don't worry. We're not giving up, we're just taking a little break in the action."

"Very well," Momma said as we both spied a pile of pipes and wiring on the grass in front of the cottage.

"Brace yourself," I told my mother, trying to steel myself at the same time. "This could get ugly."

"The truth is that it's not as bad as I imagined it was going to be," I admitted. The men had pulled out much of the outdated plumbing from the wall, and a good bit of the wiring as well. There was still more to do in the realm of demolition, so at least they were taking their time.

"Thanks, I think," Jake said as he surveyed the mess. "I'm worried about the kitchen, Suzanne. Look at this." He held up a piece of what appeared to be galvanized pipe.

"What exactly am I looking at?" I asked him.

"Here's what it should look like," Phillip said as he held up a shiny new section of pipe.

"Did this come out of the wall, too?"

"No, we bought it at the hardware store for illustration purposes," Jake answered. The new tube's walls were thin and expansive, whereas the old one had barely more than a pencil's diameter inside. "That's why our showers here are so weak," he said.

"What *is* that?" I asked as I studied the gunk lining the inside of the pipe section.

"Rust, mineral deposits, all kinds of things," Jake explained.

"Somebody's been on the Internet," I said with a grin.

"Hey, there's no shame in looking for more information when you know that you need it," he said a little too defensively.

"I wasn't criticizing, I was complimenting you," I quickly amended. "Do you think the kitchen pipes are like this, too?"

"There's no doubt in my mind," Jake said, and then he looked at my mother. "We need your permission to go a little further in our demolition, Dot. The water and the electric are already turned off. What could it hurt to see how bad the kitchen pipes really are?"

"I think it's an excellent idea," Momma said after a few moments. "Let's be clear, though. You can remove plaster and sections of old plumbing and wiring, but you are not to touch anything structural."

"Do we at least get an extension on our deadline?" Phillip asked her.

She smiled sweetly as she said, "You do not."

Instead of being upset, her husband just laughed and looked at Jake. "Told you."

My husband shrugged. "That just means that we're in for a long night. Are you up for it, Phillip?"

"I am if you are," he said, though both men clearly had a little less enthusiasm for the project than they'd had before.

"Is there any chance of us getting something to eat?" Jake asked me.

"We can do that," I said. "Carry on."

"You heard the lady," Jake said. "Let's get to it."

As Momma and I walked across the park to retrieve my Jeep, I suggested, "Should we pop into the Boxcar and get them their dinner?"

"I thought we might go back to my cottage and make something for them," she said.

"Momma, no offense, but they're both probably getting pretty hungry. Do we really have time to whip something up?"

"You're right, of course," she said.

After a quick trip to the Boxcar Grill, we returned with hamburgers, fries, and sweet teas for all of us. The men barely managed to grunt as they consumed the food, and soon enough, we were on our way to Momma's place, and the men were back at work.

We were standing at the Jeep, still conveniently parked in front of Donut Hearts, when I heard someone calling my name softly.

I looked around to find the source, and to my surprise, Gabby Williams was standing by ReNEWed, peeking out from the back of the shop.

"Suzanne. Dot. Over here."

As she beckoned us toward her, Momma and I shared a furtive look.

Our search for Gabby might have been in vain earlier, but we were finally going to get to ask her about the scarf that was now tucked firmly into my mother's purse.

CHAPTER 9

"Where have *you* been?" Momma asked Gabby the moment the three of us were safely locked inside the back storeroom of ReNEWed. "We've been looking all over town for you."

"What Momma means to say is that we were worried about you," I said. I didn't want to rile Gabby up from the very start by scolding her, especially when she'd actually sought us out.

"I panicked, okay? I'm not particularly proud of it, but it is what it is," she said. "When you focused in on that scarf, I instantly knew that I'd made a mistake putting it out for sale."

"You were out in the middle of the night by the dunking booth, weren't you?" Momma asked her. She needed to slow down a little, but I didn't know how to tell her without causing a problem.

"Me? Nonsense. I know better than to traipse around town in the dead of night," Gabby said.

I wasn't sure why, but I believed her. "If it wasn't you, then who was it? You must know."

"I do, but I can't tell you. I was sworn to secrecy," she said, "and don't ask me again, because I'm not about to break my vow."

"Gabby, a man is dead. Need I remind you of that?" I asked her.

"The last I heard, the police didn't even know the cause of death. Has that suddenly changed?" she asked me with a glare.

"Not that we know of," I admitted. "Still, whoever had that scarf might know something and not even realize it. What possessed you to put it in the window display after you got it back from your friend?" It was a question that was burning a hole in me.

"I couldn't bring myself to bury it in back," she admitted.

"You probably should have just thrown it away altogether," Momma said softly.

"I considered it, but it's too perfect for the season, you know? I just couldn't bring myself *not* to sell it," she admitted. "It's too ingrained in me to get every last dime that I can out of my inventory, and this was the perfect time to sell it. Besides, who would have dreamed that someone could have spotted it?"

"Someone *did*, though. It *is* rather distinctive," I reminded her. "Your friend could be in trouble. You realize that, don't you? If they didn't have anything to do with what happened to that man, they may have seen who did without realizing its significance. It's important that they come forward." I was acting on the assumption that Carson Winfield had been murdered, but what choice did I have? If he'd died of natural causes, as unlikely as it seemed to me, then this was all for naught.

"I'm telling you, I can't say a word," Gabby said, her voice choking a little as she spoke. Was this stalwart woman about to break down and cry right in front of us?

Momma moved in deftly, and before I realized what was happening, she had wrapped Gabby up in her arms. "You can trust us, Gabrielle. You know that." There was the use of her full first name again, but this time it had been meant to comfort, not to scold her.

"Of course I know it. A promise is a promise, though. The problem is that my friend knew the victim. They were supposed to meet him at the clock, but instead, when they got there, they discovered that he was dead. Can you blame them for not wanting to admit it, given the circumstances?" She'd been careful to use the pronoun "they" instead of "him" or "her." I wasn't exactly pleased with myself, but I knew that I needed to work on her a little harder.

It was time to give her a bit of a nudge.

"How did they know Carson Winfield?" I asked, repeating her use of "they." "He's certainly not a local."

"How do you know his name?" Gabby asked me incredulously.

I wasn't about to admit that we'd stumbled across his wallet and ID stuffed into a plastic jack o'lantern nearby. "There's a great deal that we know right now," I said, mostly bluffing. "That's why your friend needs to trust us. Isn't that right, Momma?" I asked as I turned to my mother.

"There are many worse options than talking to us," my mother said, ending her hug. "At least we'll be sympathetic in a way that the police surely won't." Momma looked at me with an imploring expression, no doubt demonstrating that she was fresh out of ideas.

"Gabby, if you won't tell us your friend's identity, can you at least ask her to talk to us directly?"

"I know for a fact that she won't do that," Gabby said, and then her softness immediately stiffened. "Hang on a second. I never said that it was a woman."

"I just assumed that was the case, given the fact that the scarf is so feminine," I said, backpedaling as quickly as I could. I'd taken an educated guess, and Gabby had confirmed that it was true. In my mind, it had been worth her wrath to confirm my suspicions.

At least I hoped so, at any rate.

"Suzanne, I reached out to you for comfort, and you tricked me! I need you to leave!"

"Gabby, I didn't mean—"

"Now!" Gabby said, her voice suddenly booming.

"Suzanne, do as she asks. I'll speak with you later," Momma said. It was a good idea if it worked. If at least one of us could stay behind, perhaps Gabby would soften her position.

It was just too bad that it didn't happen that way.

"I'm sorry, Dot, but you need to go as well."

"Gabby, Suzanne didn't mean—"

The owner of ReNEWed softened her voice, but her words still carried steel in them. "I'm afraid that I must insist."

There was no room for negotiation, and Momma and I both knew it.

As we were ushered out the back door, I gave it one last shot. "Gabby, at least try to get her to come to us. We'll help her in any way that we can. Will you at least try?"

"I'm not making any promises to you right now," Gabby said firmly.

At least it wasn't a direct no.

"We didn't handle that very well, did we?" Momma asked me as we walked back to the Jeep.

"With Gabby, you take a chance every time you open your mouth," I said. "We learned a few things before she threw us out though, so it wasn't a total loss."

"I suppose," Momma admitted grudgingly.

"Come on. Cheer up. Now we know that a woman Gabby considers a close friend not only knew the dead man, but she was going to meet him at the town clock in the middle of the night. That doesn't exactly describe a casual relationship, does it? Shoot, before our conversation with Gabby, we weren't even positive that it was a woman."

"Yes, I can see all of that, but what good will it do us if Gabby's friend won't identify herself?"

"We need to identify her ourselves, then," I told Momma. "Gabby's list of friends can't be that long, can it?"

"I'd say it would be rather brief," she said.

"So we start filling in that list so we can figure out who it might be," I said.

"Do you honestly believe that someone in town killed that man, Suzanne?"

"I don't know, but I want to be ready to move in case they did," I replied. "I just can't imagine him dying of natural causes on that dunking-tank platform."

"While we're coming up with our list, would you care to bake with me? It occurs to me that the men could use something special in repayment for their labors."

I didn't usually bake as a part of my sleuthing, but then again, Momma wasn't normally my partner, either. "What did you have in mind?"

"In the spirit of the season, I thought pumpkin muffins might be in order," she said. "What do you think of that?"

"If I get half of everything that comes out of the oven, you're on," I said. My mother's pumpkin bread recipe, especially when it was converted into muffins, was one of the most amazing quick breads I'd ever had in my life.

"That's awfully greedy, isn't it?" Momma asked with a laugh, clearly pleased by my request.

"Hey, you're not the only one in the family who knows how to strike a hard bargain. What do you say?"

"You've got yourself a deal, but we divide them evenly before you've had any samples yourself," she answered.

It was a tough pill to swallow, given the fact that I liked to stuff myself with muffins the moment they were cool enough to eat. Still, half a batch of muffins was a great deal better than no muffins at all. I stuck out my hand. "Let's shake on it."

Her laughter became even heartier, but she took my hand, and we had a bargain.

It was the best deal I'd ever get, and I knew it.

"This has been fun," I said later as I surveyed the cooling pumpkin muffins now occupying three different large cooling racks on Momma's kitchen counters. I baked all morning most days when I was at Donut Hearts, but doing it with my mother was an entirely different experience. The muffins were the result of those actions, but the memories I had of our time making them outweighed the finished products by far. Every moment and experience I had with my mother was more important than any treat, no matter how good it might be.

I think.

Those muffins *were* awfully tasty.

After we delivered an even dozen pumpkin muffins to the workmen, who were more than happy to receive them, Momma and I headed back to her cottage so we could call it a night. After all, I had another big day of donut making ahead of me, and who knew what major wheeling and dealing my mother was going to undertake.

We never made it back to the cottage though, at least not without a complication that nearly wrecked us, literally.

As I drove into the growing darkness, I had to slam on the brakes immediately, bringing us to a sudden and jarring stop.

As it was, I still nearly ran over what appeared to be a dead body lying in the middle of Springs Drive.

CHAPTER 10

"**S**UZANNE, ARE YOU ALL RIGHT?" Momma asked me shakily after we were completely stopped in the middle of the road just beside the defunct railroad tracks.

As I got out of the front door to see what was lying in the road, I said, "I'm fine. How about you? Are you okay?"

"Truth be told, I'm a little rattled," Momma said as she joined me in front of my Jeep, where I was just beginning to kneel down to check the body in the road. My headlights illuminated the scene a bit eerily as I examined it a little more closely. It had been wrapped in a couple of garbage bags, and then it had been tied up with strong rope around the neck, torso, and legs.

Only it wasn't a body.

Probing the trash bags tentatively, I could feel plastic and paper yield under my touch. This was no doubt one of the dummies Officer Bradley had referred to earlier.

As I ripped the bags open, my mother said, "Suzanne, you shouldn't do that!"

"It's okay. It's just garbage, Momma," I explained. Now that the trash bags were torn open, I could see that a wide array of empty plastic milk jugs, bleach containers, wadded-up newspaper, and an assortment of other debris had been carefully shaped into the form of a body. Someone had gone to a lot of trouble to play a very dangerous prank on us. It would have been bad enough if they'd just leaned their Halloween creation against a tree or put it on a park bench, but they'd chosen to dump it in the middle of the road, where it could have easily caused an accident. Was it the same prankster who had left the mask and broom against my window earlier, or was this some other mental adolescent trying to be funny? If this was what Fright Week was going to be like, we were in for several long days.

I gathered up the garbage, now unrecognizable as a body, and put it all off to the side of the road near the donut shop. Donut Hearts had started life as a train depot, so its proximity to the tracks wasn't unexpected to anyone who knew its history.

The identity of whoever was trying to scare me was a complete mystery, however.

Or should I be taking it all so personally? Maybe I'd just been hit by pranksters twice at random, an odd coincidence that could just be explained away.

The problem was that I wasn't a big fan of coincidences.

"Do you think there's a chance this was meant specifically for us?" I asked Momma as we got back into my Jeep.

She looked shocked by the concept. "Why on earth would someone want to scare the wits out of us like that, Suzanne?"

"Isn't it clear? We're asking questions about the body I found this morning. That mask might not have been a warning, but this could certainly be interpreted as one, don't you think?"

Momma didn't answer right away. "I hate to say it, but I need to ask you a question. Is there a chance you're just being a little paranoid?"

"Oh, there's a great big whopping chance of that," I admitted. "But don't forget, being paranoid has kept me alive more than once in the past."

"The question remains, who knows we're looking into Carson Winfield's history?" Momma asked me as I reconsidered just leaving the debris by the road. On a whim, I pulled the Jeep in front of the donut shop and got out again.

As Momma followed, I said, "At this point, there are lots of people who make the cut. So far we've talked to Gabby, Trish, Jenny, and Stevie. Who knows who might have overheard one of those conversations? What if someone wants Carson Winfield's death to just go away, and this is their way of warning us off?"

"I have no idea," she said. As I started collecting the trash, Momma asked me, "Suzanne, what in the world are you doing now?"

"If this was meant to be a warning, maybe the person trying to scare us off slipped up and included something personal in the parts that make up this body," I said. "Give me a hand, would you?"

Momma shrugged and dove right in beside me. I loved that about her. She could take someone else's idea and run with it, and she wasn't afraid to get her hands dirty, either. I opened the back of the donut shop, got an oversized trash bag of my own, and stuffed everything into it. I'd look through it later, but for now, it would be safe.

After we'd washed our hands, we locked the shop's back door and headed out front.

To my surprise, Chief Grant was standing beside my Jeep, waiting for us with a grim look on his face.

"I've got news. It turns out that it was murder after all," he said simply. "Someone shoved a long, sharp needle into Carson Winfield's heart."

CHAPTER 11

"WHAT? ARE YOU SURE? IF he was stabbed to death, then why didn't I see any blood?" I asked, having seen the body myself several hours earlier.

"The wooden needle broke off in his chest when he was stabbed, and evidently the tip of it was still in him," the chief explained. "That's what stopped the blood from flowing out. The man's chest was so hairy that I missed the needle fragment completely when I examined him, but the coroner found it soon enough."

"What kind of needle was it? Do you happen to know?" Momma asked.

"It's one generally used for knitting, I believe," the chief answered, looking a bit perplexed by my mother's question. "Why? Does it matter?"

"Wooden knitting needles are often used by older folks who have joint pain. They are lighter and require less tension than metal ones," she explained. "Whoever used it on the victim could be older or have arthritis."

"How do you know so much about knitting needles?" I asked Momma, forgetting the police chief for a moment.

"*I* know things too, Suzanne," she said with the hint of a frown. Then, turning back to the police chief, Momma added, "I would think that one of those needles would be difficult to break off. I've seen them before, and they've always felt quite stout to me."

"That's the thing," the police chief explained. "Whoever did it cut a thin kerf all the way around the needle. My guess is that it was modified to be a murder weapon from the start, so that makes it premeditated. Whoever met the victim this morning knew they were going to kill him before they even got to the town clock for their rendezvous."

"So, do you believe the killer likes to knit?" I asked my mother.

"Perhaps, or maybe they stumbled across the needle and decided to use it for something besides its intended purpose."

"Then again, they could have picked one up at a friend's place, or bought one not caring what it had been originally designed for," the chief added.

"I don't see how that's possible," I said. "Knitting needles are not exactly an impulse purchase. Besides, there are lots of things that could be used to stab someone in the heart."

"Suzanne," Momma scolded me.

"Well, it's true. I can think of several different things that could have been used instead, like an ice pick, a metal skewer, or even a tent stake, and those are just off the top of my head."

"Maybe so, but all of those things would have generated a great deal of blood loss if the weapon were removed, and if they were left in, the cause of death would have been immediately obvious," the chief said.

"So then you believe that whoever did it wanted the crime to go undetected for as long as possible," I said. "If that's true, why kill Carson when he was perched on the dunking-booth platform? It's not exactly the most inconspicuous place in town, is it?"

"I have no idea, but I'll be sure to ask the killer after I catch them," the chief said. "Anyway, I thought you'd like to know. I figured that it was the least I could do."

"Not really. The least you could have done was not tell us a thing," I corrected him. "We appreciate it."

"I figured I owed you at least that much," he said. "Has anything exciting happened with you lately?"

I was certain that Momma was about to tell him, but I wasn't sure I wanted to share the news about the dummy "body" we'd found in the street.

"We made pumpkin muffins," I said, cutting Momma off and hoping she would take the hint.

Unfortunately, it sailed right over her head. "Suzanne, have you already forgotten about the body we found just a few minutes ago?"

"What? A body?" the chief asked, his voice raised in agitation. "What are you talking about, Dot?"

"It wasn't really a body," I explained, giving my mother an icy stare. If she noticed it, she failed to comment on it or to react to it in any way at all. "Someone went to a lot of trouble to arrange trash in a pair of garbage bags to look like a body."

"I *hate* pranks," the chief said. "Where is it now?"

"It's in the back of Donut Hearts," Momma volunteered, "but Suzanne already tore it up."

"Hey, I had my reasons," I explained. "I thought it might be a real body at first."

"Where exactly did you find it?" he asked Momma, ignoring me completely. Who could blame him, really? Momma had turned out to be a wealth of information, after all.

"It was lying in the road," she said. "Suzanne nearly wrecked the Jeep trying not to run it over."

"Honestly, it wasn't that bad. I thought it was real, but it just turned out to be a prank gone bad," I explained.

"Let's see it," the chief said as he started walking toward the back of the shop.

"I'm sure it was just meant to be a joke," I explained. I wanted to examine that trash myself, not turn it over to the police.

"When whoever did it left it in the middle of the road, the joke ended," he said. "I'm going to do my best to figure out who's responsible, and they're going to pay for their prank."

There was no talking him out of it, so once he collected the remnants of the "body" we'd nearly run over, the chief left.

"Did you have to tell him *everything*?" I asked her.

"But I didn't! I didn't say one word about Gabby's friend," my mother said, clearly feeling a little offended by my accusation.

That was just too bad. "Momma, I wanted to study that trash myself."

"Suzanne, you said it yourself. There are things we need to let the police handle," she said, actually scolding me a little. Why did I suddenly feel like I was the one who had just messed up?

"In the future, I'd appreciate it if you'd let *me* decide what we tell the police and what we hold back," I said as calmly as I could manage.

"I'm not sure I can agree to that," Momma said a little stiffly.

I knew there was no point arguing with her, so I decided to drop it for the moment. "Fine. Let's go back to your cottage. I'm tired, and I have to get up early tomorrow to make donuts."

"You work too hard," Momma said, a common theme for her scolding.

"The truth is that I work exactly as hard as I have to," I said. "If anything, you're the workaholic in the family, not me."

"Suzanne, what I do is not work. It's fun," she said.

The stress of her life would kill me in a month, and I knew it. I hated the idea of buying and selling properties, turning them over while always striving to make a profit, but it really was a game for her. "Whatever," I said, not caring to discuss it anymore.

"I hate that phrase," Momma said. "But 'no problem' is even worse. What has happened to our language?"

"I don't know, Momma," I said, "and I'm too tired to talk about it right now."

All I wanted was a long, hot shower and some sleep before it was time to get up and make donuts again.

I was barely aware of it when Jake came to bed, and not much later, I gathered up my clothes, tiptoed out of the bedroom, took a quick shower, and then I went into the kitchen to grab a bite of something before I had to go to work.

Momma was up and waiting for me, something I'd been half expecting based on past experience. There was a bowl of oatmeal on the table for me, as well as a large glass of orange juice. As a rule I wasn't a fan of oatmeal for breakfast, or any time of day for that matter, but Momma managed to make it taste special. I'd never been able to duplicate it at home, and she'd been reticent to share her secret, no matter how much I'd asked.

"Thanks for breakfast," I said after I finished, rinsed out my bowl, and put it into the dishwasher. "It was sweet of you to get up."

"I was more than happy to do it, my dear, sweet child," Momma said as she kissed my cheek. "Have a good day, and don't do any sleuthing without me."

"I'll try my best to resist the urge," I said, and then I was off, making my way to the donut shop in the dark, wondering what new things this day was about to bring me.

When Emma came in, she immediately handed me a folded newspaper. "It's hot off the presses, and I thought you might like a copy." It was *The April Springs Sentinel*, her father's paper. A large photo of the dead man, Carson Winfield, occupied much of the space above the fold. Over his photo was one word, written in large black letters. MURDER.

It was enough to incite a riot, and I was sure that George and Cassandra would have fits when they saw it. Somehow Ray Blake must have had an inside source at the police department. I sincerely doubted that Chief Grant had told him the news personally.

"Your dad isn't afraid to make a splash, is he?" I asked as I read the article below the fold. It appeared that Carson Winfield had once lived in Union Square, a town not thirty minutes away from us. I'd been wondering about his connections with April Springs, so that could partially explain his presence here. But why kill him now, and in such a convoluted way? Unfortunately, the newspaper was rather sparse on those particular details, not that it kept Ray from speculating on all kinds of things, including the odd choice of location where I'd found Carson's body. According to one of Ray's theories, the murder victim had been attacked by a clown who'd been offended by him being on the dunking-tank bench, at least that was what the story implied. Then again, in the next paragraph, Ray suggested that it might have been, in no particular order, a casual acquaintance, an old buddy from high school, a jilted lover from his past, or an alien from outer space. No doubt his theories might sell newspapers, but they would do nothing to help solve the man's murder.

"Will they cancel Fright Week now?" Emma asked me as she started in on the first round of dishes, bowls, plates, and utensils.

"I have no idea," I said as I started the second round of my work, creating the raised donuts that would soon complement the cake ones I'd already made.

"Surely you have a guess, though," she said.

"If I had to say, I'm willing to bet that it will go on as planned, despite the murder," I said, knowing that it was probably true. The town, the mayor, and his girlfriend all had too much invested in the festivities to just let it all vanish. Short of something happening in front of eyewitnesses at high noon to someone prominent in town, I believed that Fright Week would go on.

"I hope you're right. After all, we have the first round of our donut-decorating contest this morning. Should I start getting ready for that?"

"No, let's wait and see what happens," I said. "I could be wrong, you know."

"You could be, but I doubt it," she said. "Tell you what. I'll knock out these dishes, and then we can take our break together."

"That sounds good to me," I said, though I wasn't looking forward to going outside, even with her company. A little less than twenty-four hours before, I'd stumbled across Carson Winfield's body, and there was a part of me that didn't ever want to take another break outside again. Then again, I couldn't let it keep me from living my life.

Soon enough, it was time for our break. I covered the mixer's bowl full of the dough to give it a chance to proof, and I turned to Emma. She was nearly finished with the dirty dishes.

"Ready?" I asked her as I set my timer.

"You know, we really don't have to go outside," Emma said, no doubt sensing my reluctance.

"Nonsense. You know the rules; we take our break outside in rain and even snow."

"Are you sure?" The concern in her voice was obvious.

"I'm positive," I said, thankful that I had such a good employee, and a great friend to boot.

"Then grab a jacket. It's chilly out there," Emma said, doing her best to ramp up her enthusiasm.

"You don't have to tell me," I said as we started for the door. "I came in before you did, remember?"

"Emma, was this here when you came in this morning?" I asked her, holding up a plastic jack o'lantern treat bucket identical to the one I'd found Carson Winfield's clothes in.

"I don't think so, but I could be wrong," Emma said with a shrug. "On the drive over here this morning, I saw them all over town. I'm not surprised, since they gave them away at the grocery store last night to kids under nine."

I approached the treat bucket cautiously, holding my breath as I peered inside.

Thankfully, it was empty.

Letting my heartbeat get back to normal, I put the jack o'lantern near the trash can and took my seat at the outdoor table where we always took our breaks.

Emma reached into her coat and pulled out something wrapped in foil. "I nearly forgot all about this."

She handed the package to me, and as I started to unwrap it, I saw that it was a donut. "Gee, thanks, but I don't really want a donut right now. No offense."

Emma grinned. "Finish unwrapping it, Suzanne."

I did as she asked, and I saw that the donut wasn't the usual round variety. Instead, it was a modified ellipse, with a stem on top and an indentation at the bottom. "It's a pumpkin," she said, smiling. "Imagine it decorated in orange icing with eyes and a mouth iced in black. It could be a real hit with our customers."

I glanced over at the grinning jack o'lantern near the trash and felt a shiver go through me. "Where did you get this?"

"I found it online," she admitted, finally noticing my

uneasiness. "Suzanne, we don't have to use it. I just thought it might be a hoot for the contest. We can make plain yeast donuts for that if you'd rather."

"No, this is better," I said. "It shouldn't waste much dough, either. Do you have the cutter with you?"

"It's inside, waiting to be washed. Man, that thing really has you spooked, doesn't it?" Emma asked as she walked over and picked the jack o'lantern up. "It's just a piece of plastic. See?" As Emma flipped it around end over end, she glanced down at it, and then she stopped suddenly.

"What is it? What's wrong?" I asked her.

"Suzanne, there's something written on the bottom of it," Emma said as she handed it to me.

Written in black magic marker was one word, printed in neat block letters.

STOP.

"What does *that* mean? Is it directed at us, or is it just some random word printed there? If it is meant for us, are we supposed to stop the contest, stop participating in Fright Week, or stop making donuts altogether? This can't be meant for us," Emma said, dismissing it entirely.

"There's something else you should know," I said. "Yesterday morning when I took my break, someone leaned a broomstick up against the front glass with a pumpkin mask on it. Then yesterday someone threw their garbage shaped like a body in the road, and I almost ran over it. These can't be coincidences."

"Suzanne, people are playing pranks all over town. Jan Kerber had her car windows soaped, and someone put a Styrofoam tombstone in front of our place. Emily told me that she got hit, too. Some genius painted a huge black cat on the front of Cow,

Spots, and Moose with the same kind of paint I used to decorate ours."

I hadn't heard about that, and somehow the news made me feel a bit better. "What did she do, just wash it off?"

"No, she decided to use it instead, so she painted images of the three guys riding it like cowboys. It's really kind of cute. She even painted little cowboy hats on all three of them. Don't take this personally. It's just somebody's bad idea of a joke."

Maybe Emma was right. If people were getting pranked all over town, what had been done to me hadn't been anything special. It didn't help that my paranoia levels were ramped up to maximum. Still, I decided to keep the jack o'lantern, just in case.

"Are we holding onto that?" Emma asked a few minutes later when my timer went off, signaling that the dough was ready for its next phase.

"I thought I might keep it for now," I said. "I made nearly twice the dough for the contest. If no one shows up, we're going to be throwing away dozens and dozens of donuts."

"Don't worry. Every kid in town is going to want to do it, especially since they get to eat their works of art after the judging is over. Are George and Cassandra still picking the winners?"

"You'd better believe it. I have no desire to disappoint all of the kids who lose."

"It's brave of them to do it then, isn't it?" Emma asked.

"I'm not sure I'd call it bravery. I'm just glad that *we* don't have to make any decisions," I said. "Now, let's see that cutter. I hope it's strong enough to hold up."

"It's going to be fine. Mom and I made a full practice run last night."

I stopped in my tracks. "I thought you just made one so you

could show me. Are you telling me that you made donuts on your one day off from your job making donuts?"

"It does sound crazy when you put it like that," Emma conceded.

"My friend, you've got the donut-making bug as bad as I do," I said with a laugh, forgetting the murder for a moment, but just a moment.

It was hard not to let it creep back into my thoughts though, and by the time we were ready to open to the public, I'd found myself having a hard time thinking of anything else.

CHAPTER 12

"**S**O, IT WAS MURDER AFTER all," Mattie Jones said after she ordered a pumpkin-shaped donut. We'd held back four dozen for the contest, but that had still left us plenty to sell to the general public, and they were a big hit. I hadn't added eyes and teeth to all of them, and to my surprise, they'd sold well, too. Who knew what the public would like and what they would turn their noses up at. I'd made donuts in the past that I thought were sure winners, only to be rejected by my customers. Some I hadn't thought good enough to even sell, but Emma had convinced me otherwise, and a few of them had even made it into our regular rotation.

"That's what I understand," I said as I gave her change, and then I noticed her shawl. "Did you knit that yourself?"

"I did. It's nice, isn't it?" she asked as she twirled around.

"I didn't know you were a knitter," I said.

"I used to be, but I gave it up after I made this. You know me. I become obsessed with something, and it's all I can think about, then I grow bored and switch my attention to something else. Right now it's cooking in a wok. You should come by and I'll make you something sometime."

"Maybe," I said, filing away the information.

"You're digging into the crime, aren't you?" Mattie asked in a conspiratorial voice spoken so softly that only I could hear.

"What makes you ask that?"

"Come on, Suzanne. Nobody could blame you, given that

you found the poor man. Was there much blood?" she asked a little too ghoulishly for my taste.

"I can't really talk about it," I said, trying not to be too curt to someone who was slowly going from being an infrequent customer to a regular one.

Mattie misunderstood, reading "can't" as being "not allowed to." After nodding briefly, she said, "The police don't want you spreading things around. I get it. Well, good luck."

I thought about stopping her and correcting her, but a line was forming, and I didn't really want to get into it with her in front of everyone else there. As usually happened when I was involved in a murder investigation, my customers seemed to come out in droves. I was sure they were all hoping for some insights into the crime, some behind-the-scenes tidbits I might share with them, but I did my best not to get into it, especially when I was actively investigating a case.

"What can I get for you today?" I asked Arthur Bradshaw as he approached the counter, next in line.

"Got any more of those eyeballs?" he asked.

I'd made quite a few more, but they'd been going at a brisk pace, despite their creepy nature. "I don't have any blues left, but I have two browns, a green, and one that's bloodshot."

"I'll take 'em all," he said with a grin.

After I bagged them up, being careful to place them in the bottom of the bag without smudging the icing any more than I had to, I took his money and waited for the inevitable questioning to begin.

He didn't say a word about me finding the body though, and that fact made me a bit curious. "Aren't you going to ask me about Carson Winfield?" I asked him.

Arthur frowned, shook his head, and then he left abruptly, forgetting his donut holes *and* his change. "Arthur, you forgot your money and your donuts."

"Sorry. I thought I heard someone calling my name outside," he explained as he quickly came back to the counter, grabbed the donut holes, shoved the change into the tip jar, and then took off.

That was odd behavior, even given the circumstances. Arthur was usually pretty inquisitive by nature. So why was he quiet about Carson Winfield's murder? I'd have to look into his reticence once I had more time, and Mattie Jones might bear investigating as well. Not only was she a knitter, but she was taking an awfully active interest in the murder.

I had to laugh at myself. Mattie was a suspect because she asked too many questions, and Arthur was one because he didn't. Maybe I was getting a little too carried away thinking that anyone around me could have done it. I'd need to back off a little before I blew a fuse.

I wouldn't be able to do it just yet, though, because Gabby Williams was storming toward my donut shop, clearly furious about something.

"Suzanne, I need to have a word with you," she said, barely acknowledging anyone else in my shop.

"I'm kind of busy right now, Gabby," which was true enough, but I really didn't want to talk to her when she was so upset. If I could stall her for a while, maybe she'd have a chance to cool off before we spoke.

Then again, probably not, but it was at least worth a shot.

Gabby wasn't about to be thwarted, though.

"Right now, Suzanne. Get your assistant up here. That's what she's for, isn't it?"

I knew that there was no room for negotiation in her voice. "Let me get Emma." After my assistant had taken over the front counter, I put a hand on Gabby's arm. She recoiled from my touch, something that didn't make me feel particularly hopeful about the coming conversation. "Let's step into the kitchen," I suggested. For one thing, it was my home turf, so maybe I'd feel a little better about our pending conversation. For another, if we stepped outside, I was certain several of my customers would relocate with us, hoping to overhear our discussion. I didn't think the folks of April Springs were particularly nosy, but they certainly weren't shy about trying to overhear something that might be juicy and, just as important, repeatable.

"Fine. I don't care where we talk, just as long as we talk."

We walked in back, and as I passed Emma, she gave me a quick look of sympathy.

I was afraid that I was going to need it.

"Now, what's so important?" I asked her, deciding to meet fire with fire. If she was going to be aggressive about our conversation, then I would be, too.

"You just had to go behind my back and start harassing her, didn't you?" she asked angrily. "I don't know how you figured out who she was, but you clearly managed it somehow."

I didn't even have to play dumb, since I had no idea what she was talking about. "Do you mind explaining yourself a little more? I'm afraid that I'm lost."

"Suzanne, it's not going to work with me. Margaret told me that someone painted a black cat on her front door. It was you, wasn't it?"

"Margaret? *She's* the one you've been protecting?" I asked, surprised by Gabby's willingness to tell me a secret that she'd been guarding so closely just the day before.

"You really didn't know, did you?" Gabby asked as she reached into her pocket and pulled out a small talisman, a knitted elephant, and started to play with it absently as she spent a few moments in thought. "Oh, no, I've made a terrible mistake. Forget I said anything."

Gabby started for the door, but I blocked her exit, a dangerous move even if she wasn't agitated, which she clearly was at the moment. "I'm really sorry, but I can't do that. Margaret was meeting Carson yesterday morning, wasn't she?"

"Yes," Gabby said, clearly furious with herself for divulging the information and now squeezing the poor little animal even tighter. "She didn't kill him, though."

I wasn't about to debate that fact with Gabby. "Momma and I need to speak with her."

"Suzanne, I was supposed to protect her, and all I've done is make a mess of things! How can I arrange for you to grill her about something that's too painful for her to talk about? I'm her best friend, and she won't tell me anything about it!"

"Find a way to persuade her, then," I said calmly.

Evidently she took it the wrong way. "Are you *threatening* me, Suzanne?" Gabby asked. Was she actually happy that she had somewhere to redirect her anger? I wasn't backing down, though. I couldn't afford to, given the circumstances.

"Gabby, it's not a threat; it's a promise. Margaret either talks to us willingly, or we push her until she has no choice but to comply with our request. Someone's been painting black cats on windows all over town. You're just being paranoid, but I understand why. I know you two are friends, and we won't make it any harder on Margaret than we have to, but we need to speak with her about Carson Winfield, and sooner rather than later. I can guarantee you one thing, though; we'll be gentler with her than the police will be."

"You just know they'll want to talk to her, too," Gabby argued. Was her resolve cracking just a little? I hoped so. Going against Gabby Williams always left me exhausted and shaking, and normally I avoided it at almost any cost if I could help it.

Clearly this was the exception.

I had no choice.

"She has one chance to avoid that," I said.

"How is that possible?"

"If Momma and I solve this murder before the police find out about her involvement in the case, her name will never come up."

"Are you really saying that you wouldn't tell your buddy, the police chief?" Gabby asked, surprised by my admission.

"Only if we run out of options," I said. What had I just promised? If Chief Grant found out that I'd been holding out on him, he wouldn't be at all happy with me. Then again, I had to give up *something* to get Gabby on my side. Margaret would be a tough nut to crack without Gabby backing us, and I knew it.

"I need your word, Suzanne."

"I give you my word that I'll do my best to keep her name out of this," I said, the only concession I could really make. "I'm sorry. I know you want more, but I'm not going to lie to you."

Gabby seemed to consider that, and after a moment, she nodded. "Okay. I suppose that's the best I'm going to get from you. Come by ReNEWed after you close at eleven. We'll be in back waiting for you."

"What about your customers?" I asked her.

"I'll close the store," she said. "This is too important."

"Fine. We'll see you then. Thanks for making this happen, Gabby."

The shop owner looked at me fiercely, and then she said, "I'm doing this for Margaret, not for you, Suzanne."

"I understand," I said, still feeling the sting of her words.

Gabby was about to leave when I asked, "Where did you get that elephant? Did you knit it yourself?"

"Do I look like a knitter?" she asked me. "It was a gift."

"From whom?" I asked her, not backing down for one second.

"None of your business," she answered abruptly.

"It was from Margaret, wasn't it?" I asked, taking a stab in the dark.

"She finds knitting them relaxing," Gabby admitted. "You can't use that against her, though. I heard how that man died. Just because she knits doesn't make her a murderer, Suzanne."

"I never thought it did," I replied. It didn't exactly rule her out, either.

"Fine then," Gabby said, and then she started toward the door yet again.

As we walked out of my kitchen together, Gabby eschewing creeping out the backdoor like some kind of scoundrel, all eyes were on us, but no one dared to speak a word. Things were quiet for five seconds after Gabby left, and then the normal droning buzz of conversation took back over. Emma resumed her duties in back, and I took my place at the counter. It was as normal as things could possibly be, given the circumstances, but I for one reveled in the opportunity to sell donuts and not dig into a stranger's murder.

Unfortunately, my customers had other ideas.

"You the chick that found Carson?" a gruff man asked me fifteen minutes later as he walked up to the counter.

"I am the woman who discovered his body, that is correct. Who are you?" I wasn't usually so blunt with my customers, but this man had irritated me from the moment he called me a chick. His chin sported sporadic gray whiskers, and his hair was in serious need of a trim. I couldn't tell much about his clothes because he wore a long black overcoat, a duster that was clearly in need of dry cleaning. I wasn't a snob, so the state of his appearance wouldn't have bothered me if it hadn't been for his attitude.

"I'm Carson's only friend in the world," the man said, though if he'd felt any affection for the dead man at all, or sorrow for his loss, he wasn't showing it to me.

"Good for you," I said, finding myself matching his manner.

"Say, you treat all of your customers like this?" he asked me, the edge growing in his voice.

"That's the thing. You're not a customer."

"Why do you say that?"

"Because you haven't ordered anything," I answered, pointing out the obvious.

"Give me a donut, then," he said.

"What kind would you like?"

"Surprise me," he said.

If I'd had any that were old and stale, that was what I would have served him. Instead, I had to be satisfied with a lemon-filled donut that most of the filling had already oozed out of. I needn't have been so careful in selecting my worst to offer him. After he slid the money across the counter to me, he jammed the entire donut into his mouth and downed it as though it were a contest.

I doubted that he'd even tasted it.

"Now I'm a customer. Tell me about it."

I shook my head. "You must have misunderstood me. Your purchase entitled you to a donut, not a question-and-answer session with the owner," I said.

"Okay. I get it." He reached into his wallet and pulled out a twenty. "Does that buy me some of your time?"

I was tired of playing this game with him. I touched the bill and slid it back across the counter toward him. "Sorry. I don't know anything that could be useful to you. I was taking a walk on my break when I found your friend. I called the police, and that's all I know."

"Okay, I get that," he said as he retrieved the bill. "If you don't know anything about Carson, who would?"

"Have you tried asking the police?" I asked him.

The stranger looked at me as though I'd suggested he operate on himself without anesthesia. "The thing is, the cops and me don't get along so good," he said. "Anybody else I could talk to?"

"Sorry I can't help you."

"Gotcha. Okay then."

As he started to leave, I called out, "I never caught your name."

Instead of answering, he just grinned back at me. "That could be because I didn't give it."

The second he was gone, I called Chief Grant. "A man was just at the donut shop asking about Carson Winfield. He claims to have been his only friend in the world, and when I asked him what his name was, he refused to give it to me. He was wearing a dark duster like a trench coat, and he has gray hair and stubble in need of a shave."

"Got it," the chief said. "Thanks."

It wasn't my problem anymore.

Let the chief handle him.

I had things to do myself.

CHAPTER 13

"I WASN'T SURE YOU WERE GOING to show up," I told George and Cassandra as they came into the donut shop a few minutes before we were going to get set up for the first donut-decorating contest. "I thought I was going to have to do the judging myself."

"We wouldn't have done that to you," George said. "But I don't see what the problem is. Would it have been so bad if we hadn't made it?"

I took a deep breath before I replied and let it out slowly. "Mayor, there's going to be one winner, and the rest are going to be losers. Let that be on your heads, not mine," I said.

"Perhaps we didn't think this through, dear," Cassandra told him.

"Nonsense. They all know the nature of the contest going in. It will be fine."

"We'll still be having it, then?" I asked him.

"Of course we are. Why wouldn't we?" George asked.

"I thought that when the police discovered that it was murder, you might start shutting things down," I admitted.

"There's nothing we can do for that poor man," Cassandra said. "And you know what they say. The show must go on."

"If you say so," I said, trying to keep my voice level.

George noticed something in my tone, though. "Suzanne, can I see you in the kitchen for a second? Cassandra, why don't you help Emma and the others get things set up out here?"

"Are you sure you don't need me?" she asked him as she glanced in my direction.

"Thanks, but I've got it covered," George said.

"Listen, before you start in on me," I said the second we were alone, "You should know that I'm doing the best I can with her."

"Really? That's your *best*?" he asked me in the way only good friends are willing to do. It was clear that he didn't worry too much about offending me and that I didn't have to worry that much, either. "I kind of think you can do better than that. She's a fine woman, Suzanne, and she's going to be a part of my life and this town, so you might as well get used to it."

"Have things really gotten that serious between you?" I asked him.

"That's the direction they're heading," he admitted. "So, what's your problem? The entire town is suddenly acting like I've done something wrong."

"Do you want to know the truth, or do you want me to sugarcoat it for you?"

"Do you even have to ask?" George asked me, doing his best not to get angry. He might have learned some diplomacy skills since he'd become mayor, but the raw, rough George was clearly still there, lurking just beneath the surface.

"Stop letting Cassandra run April Springs," I said.

The mayor looked at me sharply, and then, after a moment, he said softly, "She's not running it. I'm the one in charge."

I eased my tone to match his. I'd said it in an inflammatory way on purpose so I could get his attention. Now we could chat like two old friends. "If that's really the truth, then it wouldn't hurt to show people that. It's okay to consult with her, but *you* need to be the public face of this town. We elected you, George, not her. Most folks seemed to like her just fine before Fright Week, but she's losing the chance to make friends left and right with the way she's been acting lately."

The mayor took that in as well, and then, after a few moments, he nodded. "Okay. I get it. I'll talk to her. You'll like her if you give her a chance, Suzanne. I just know it."

"I'm looking forward to getting the opportunity," I said. "As long as she doesn't try to tell me what to do, we'll be fine."

"She wouldn't do that," George protested.

"Why wouldn't she? She's doing it to you," I countered.

"I said I'd talk to her," George said as he started to walk out of the kitchen. Did I have to offend everyone who came into the donut shop to speak with me? Apparently so.

I followed the mayor out and saw George take his girlfriend's arm and walk her out the door.

"What did you say to him?" Emma asked me.

"We had a much-needed chat, that's all," I said. "Why?"

"When you two came out from the kitchen, he looked as though he'd just been to the principal's office," Emma said.

I wasn't about to get into my conversation with the mayor. "What do we need to do to get set up in here?"

"For one thing, this won't work," Emma said.

"Why not? We still have plenty of donuts to decorate and all of the toppings there are," I said as I glanced back at our inventory.

"The problem is that there are fifty kids out there preregistering for the contest," she said. "Barton is taking names and giving out numbers, and my mom and dad are getting tables and chairs from City Hall."

"Tell them they don't need the chairs. The kids can decorate standing up," I said as I looked outside.

Emma was right. The town was crawling with kids ready to adorn their own donuts.

"Good idea," she said as she grabbed her phone and made the call.

By the time we got the tables up, the police chief had temporarily blocked Springs Drive from Grace's place all the way to City Hall. Anyone who had any business anywhere in between would have to do it on foot. The long folding tables were quickly set up, the tablecloths taped down, and the paper plates brought out, though not yet distributed.

"Thanks for coming," I said, trying three times to get everyone's attention but failing miserably.

Finally Chief Grant blew a whistle so loudly that all conversations stopped instantly. He grinned at me as he nodded and said, "Go ahead."

I tried not to laugh as I said, "Welcome to the first round of Fright Week's Decorate a Donut contest. This round is for kids nine and under." A few tweens grumbled at that, but I was adamant that only the youngest got to participate in this division. "The seniors competition will be held right afterwards, and the adult division will be judged tomorrow. Immediately after that, the winners from each category and each round will compete for the grand prize, a free donut a week for a year." There were several cheers from the crowd. Emma and I had played with the idea of a donut a day earlier, but that wouldn't be good for our bottom line, or our winner's bottom, either.

"Everyone participating needs to find a place at one of the tables. We will distribute the basic donuts as soon as everyone is ready. They have all been iced with a simple white icing, so don't be afraid to use your imagination." As I spoke, Emma, Sharon, Ray, and Barton put out the decorations, from small baggies half full of icing and ready to pipe to black and orange sprinkles, worm gummies, crumbled black cookies, and a dozen other odds and ends that we thought might be creepy enough to use. "We will begin in one minute."

I rolled the cart of donuts to the door and prepared to face our competitors. I was surprised to find that the kids were remarkably well behaved. I only hoped that the older participants followed suit later. As Emma and Barton put out the plates in front of the kids, Sharon and I distributed the donuts almost as quickly. We had to eject a few obvious teenagers during the process, and everyone laughed as they slunk away.

"Ready. Set. Go," I called out in a loud, strong voice.

It was an instant disaster as pandemonium reigned.

What had started off as such a good idea had quickly devolved into a donut-decorating nightmare.

The chief blew his whistle again and again, but it didn't help. Several of the kids were fighting for the same bowl of gummy worms, while another group had upended three bowls of sprinkles, which were skittering all over the pavement. Some of the kids had abandoned their donuts completely and were throwing toppings at each other, and one even hurled her donut at a rival, hitting the poor little girl in the face.

I decided that it was time to take matters into my own hands and end this before it got even uglier.

"YOUR TIME IS UP," I shouted. "Put down your toppings and step away from your donuts!" I tried to make it sound as positive and cheerful as I could, but the strain in my voice was clear.

The contest had lasted less than one minute.

"But I'm not finished," a little girl whined, obviously on the brink of tears.

I could relate.

I was on the edge of hysteria myself.

"Okay, let's see what we've got," the mayor said as he studied the carnage, doing his best to put a positive spin on things himself. Half the donuts had barely been decorated, while many had been altered beyond recognition, even given the short amount of time the kids had. How the mayor was going to choose any winners at all was beyond me. As some of the parents began to grumble, the mayor did his best to keep his smile. I looked at Cassandra, who had her face in her hands. It was clear she wasn't at all sure what to do, either, but at least she was letting the mayor handle things on his own.

For all I knew, it might have been done at random, but George quickly awarded the three winners, one for the spookiest, one for the funniest, and one for the most creative.

They all looked perilously equal to me, but before anyone could protest, George's voice boomed out, "Contestants, you may now eat your donuts!"

The kids tore into them with ravenous delight, destroying the evidence of any differences there might have been in their decorations. It was a brilliant move, and the grumbling mostly stopped as the kids squealed in delight as they consumed their donuts. Given how the contest had started, it was as good an outcome as I could have hoped for.

It had been a debacle, and what was worse, once we got everything cleaned up, we had to do it all over again.

I just hoped the seniors behaved better than the kids did, but I wasn't putting any money on it.

"Hey, Suzanne. That was really something, wasn't it?" Barton Gleason asked me as I surveyed the reset.

"Something like a disaster, you mean?" I asked him.

"Honestly, it turned out better than I thought it would," the young chef said with a grin.

I looked at him askance. "Please tell me you're joking."

"Hey, no offense. I didn't mean anything by it," Barton said, quickly backpedaling. "I still think it was a good idea. The kids had a good time, and that's really all that matters, isn't it?"

"I suppose so." I knew that we needed to talk about the restaurant idea, but I wasn't in any shape to do it at the moment.

Still, I didn't want the issue clouding things between us, so we might as well discuss it. "About the idea that you could use Donut Hearts as a restaurant," I started to say before Barton interrupted me.

"No worries. We can talk about it later," he said lightly.

"I just wanted you to know that I'm still thinking about it," I went on. "Is that okay with you?"

"Suzanne, I'm honored that you are even considering it. Now, let's get back to the task at hand. What can we do differently this time?"

"I think the plan itself was solid," I said, relieved that I didn't have to get into our joint usage of Donut Hearts at the moment. "Hopefully the seniors will be a little more disciplined than the kids were, don't you think?"

"You might think so, but you never know," he said with a smile. "When are we going to get started?"

"I'm waiting for the mayor to come back so he can judge again," I said. He and Cassandra had slipped away, and I wondered if he was going to abandon me after all. Not that I could blame him if he did. As I scanned the crowd looking for George, I saw Paige Hill, Denise Osmond, Arthur Bradshaw, Cal Jeffries, and a handful of other donut customers, but there was no sign of the mayor.

There was a tap on my shoulder, and I turned to find Max, my ex-husband, standing there grinning. "I heard about the kids' contest," he said happily. "I'm just sorry I missed it."

"Is your group going to behave any better than they did?" I asked him.

"Since when did they become 'my' group?" he asked.

"Since you took over the community theater," I said. "They all call you their ringleader."

"I just want to go on record that I'm taking no responsibility for what happens when you start the contest," Max said. "Have you seen Emily?" he asked as he looked out into the crowd. She was his steady girlfriend and one-time fiancée, but the wedding hadn't happened. They were still together though, and it wouldn't surprise me one bit if they finally got married someday.

"No, but she's about the only person from town *not* here. Look at this crowd," I said as people kept milling about, the conversations sounding like locusts from a distance.

"I know. Word got out about the kids' contest, and everyone wants to see what's going to happen now. Hey, there she is. See you later, Suzanne. Good luck."

"I'm just hoping I don't need it," I said as Max left me to join Emily.

Momma walked up at that moment and touched my arm. "Are you all right?"

"I'm as well as can be expected. Where have you been?"

"Doing some sleuthing," she said with a grin.

"Hey, you made me promise not to do anything without you. That's hardly fair that you went off on your own," I protested.

"Take a breath, Suzanne. I spent my time on the telephone, and I uncovered some pretty amazing things. It's astonishing how people will gossip once they are given the opportunity. This is turning out to be more fun than I imagined."

It was hard to be cross with her, especially since it was clear that she had made some progress on the case, which was more than I could say. "What did you find out?"

"That's all going to have to wait," Momma said as she pointed in the direction of City Hall. "Here comes the mayor and his paramour. I'll see you later."

As my mother disappeared into the crowd, I saw that George and Cassandra were indeed making their way toward me, so I decided to respect Momma's wishes and delay any further questioning, not that I had much choice. That woman was as quick as a cat when she wanted to be.

Besides, I had another contest to run.

CHAPTER 14

BEFORE GEORGE MADE IT TO me though, Jenny Preston came up. "Suzanne, have you seen Gabby or Margaret?" she asked as she scanned the crowd.

Why did everyone think that I suddenly knew where folks were? "No, but honestly, I haven't been looking for them. Why do you need them?"

"I don't. I just wanted to ask Gabby about an outfit she was holding for me, and I wanted to get Margaret's opinion on it if she was around. You know that she's been giving me a hand at the shop lately."

I'd seen Margaret Sayers working at For The Birds earlier, but contrary to popular belief, I didn't know *everything* that happened in April Springs. I assumed that Vivian Reynolds must have quit though, because I doubted that the store would need *two* clerks besides Jenny herself.

"Sorry."

"Not a problem. I'll track them down myself. Good luck," she said as she darted off into the crowd.

George finally joined me, and I noticed that Cassandra had stayed back to give him the limelight alone. I was afraid that she might be cross with me for my earlier conversation with the mayor, but when we made eye contact, she smiled and mouthed the words, "Thank you" to me, so it appeared that we were okay. Still, I'd have to make more of an effort with her, just as George had suggested. If Cassandra was going to be a big part of my friend's life, it behooved me to do my part to make her feel welcome.

"Are you ready for Round Two?" George asked me as he finally reached me. "It's quite a bigger turnout than before, isn't it?"

"I suppose bad news travels fast," I said. "Why are you so chipper?"

"Look at all these voters," George said with a grin. "How can I miss?"

"Are you *always* running for reelection, Mr. Mayor?" I asked him with a grin, glad that we were back on good terms again.

"The only way to do good is to stay on the job," George said. "I wasn't a fan of politicking in the beginning, but I've learned that it's part of what I have to do, whether I like it or not, so I might as well take advantage of it. Now, are you going to kick this thing off, or should I?"

"I'll do it," I said, surprised by how becoming mayor had changed my friend.

Stepping forward, I said in my loudest voice, "Ladies and gentlemen, thank you for coming to the seniors portion of our event. I'd like to take this moment to remind the contestants that this is all done in fun. Enjoy yourself, and don't forget, you get to eat your entry when the judging is over, so in a real way, everybody wins."

We kept the same format as the last time, and the donuts were soon distributed. We had so many contestants that we'd even had to turn a few away, much to my surprise. We could have probably jammed them in somehow, but we'd run out of donuts to decorate, something that I never thought would happen.

"Ready. Set. Go."

As I said the last word, the seniors leapt into action. There were a few squabbles about decorations, but all in all, they managed to behave themselves a sight better than the kids had. I was just about to let out the breath I was holding when it happened.

The center and largest table we'd set up suddenly collapsed, sending donuts, toppings, and seniors everywhere.

To make matters worse, one of the contestants, a gray-haired man I didn't know, fell to the ground as well, clutching his chest. The paramedics swooped in, and they soon had him on their gurney, wheeling him to the ambulance. At least he was still breathing, and he looked relatively alert. The entire time they wheeled him away, he kept shouting, "I'm fine, I tell you. I'm not having a heart attack. Somebody elbowed me in the chest when the table fell. Let me off this blasted thing."

At least there hadn't been any fatalities.

Except to my contest.

After George picked three winners in rapid succession, the crowd began to break up, leaving behind an incredible mess. Worse yet, most of the contestants didn't even eat their donuts. I hated throwing away so much food. The idea for this competition had been a disaster from start to finish, and I considered cancelling the last two events altogether, but I knew if I did that, the only thing people in April Springs would remember was that I'd reneged on a promise, and I wasn't about to let that happen. Good, bad, or indifferent, we were moving forward.

At least those contests weren't until the next day, so I'd have a little time to catch my breath.

It wasn't much, but it would have to do.

As Emma, Sharon, Barton, and I finished cleaning up, my mother approached me and said, "I checked on the men earlier."

"What men?" I asked, trying to scrape most of an iced donut off of the street.

"*Our* men," she said. "Have you already forgotten about the remodeling project?"

In the turmoil that had been surrounding me lately, I had forgotten about them indeed. "How are they doing?"

"They are both exhausted," Momma said with a grin. "If they last until dinner tonight, I'll be amazed. We're right on schedule, Suzanne."

"Well, that's something, anyway," I said. I was probably going to have to get out the garden hose to wash everything down, or we were going to have an infestation of ants that would be unprecedented for our little town.

"I thought you'd be more pleased than that," Momma said, clearly a little hurt by how her news had been received.

"I am. I just have a lot on my mind at the moment," I said.

"That's understandable enough," Momma said. I was about to ask her what she'd learned when George came up.

"Just so you know, Hiram Haskins is fine," George said.

"That's wonderful," I said. "Who exactly is Hiram Haskins?"

"The man they carted off on the stretcher," he said.

"Excellent," I said.

George just shrugged. "The volunteer fire department is going to come wash down the street any second. You've done a great job, Suzanne."

"How do you figure that?" I asked him. "The kids' contest was a nightmare, and in some ways the seniors' round was even worse."

"Maybe so, but folks are talking about it in seven counties. Turnout for Fright Week is going to go through the roof. You mark my words."

"I'm glad I could help," I said sarcastically.

"Don't take it so personally," George said. "In a month, all anybody is going to remember is that the festival was a success."

"I hope so, but I kind of doubt it," I said as I looked around. The trash had all been dealt with, the tables returned to storage, and the crowd was gone. All that was left behind was a series of sweet stains on the pavement, mostly orange blobs of icing scattered all around.

It looked as though a giant bowl of orange sherbet had exploded.

"You worry too much," George said as he waved the crew in to finish the job.

Sharon and Ray had already left, and as we gathered the trash bags together, I told Barton and Emma, "You two can take off. I'll finish up here."

"Are you sure?" Emma asked me. "I know for a fact that there are still dirty dishes inside."

"You've gone above and beyond the call of duty," I assured her. "I can handle whatever is left."

"I'll pitch in, too," Momma said.

After they were gone, we dove into the work that needed to be done, and as we did the dishes, Momma began to tell me what she'd uncovered.

"Apparently Margaret disappeared thirty years ago, and no one knew where she went. It wasn't all that uncommon for girls to visit family for extended periods of time back then," Momma said.

"Do you mean what I think you mean? Was she gone nine months?" I asked her.

"No, they'd wait until she'd started to show, but you have the right idea," Momma said.

"What does this have to do with Carson Winfield?" I asked

her as we worked side by side in the kitchen cleaning up after the mess that had been made.

"I'm not positive, but my guess is that he was the father," Momma said. "My source wasn't sure, so I've got a call in to someone else."

"Do you think Margaret killed him because of what happened so long ago?" I asked her.

"It's possible. We certainly need to speak with her about it. She's not the only one we need to talk to, though. Evidently Arthur Bradshaw and Carson had a problem a few years after that over another girl, but I'm waiting to get more details there, too."

"Wow, I've heard that revenge was a dish best served cold, but this is ridiculous. Who holds a grudge that long and then acts on it out of the blue and kills him? Why wait so long?" I asked.

"Maybe it has something to do with Carson coming back to the area," Momma said. "Evidently he lived in Montana for a good many years."

"That's got to be it, doesn't it? I can't imagine how Carson thought anything good would come of him returning to April Springs."

"He must have had his reasons, but I'm sure if he had it to do over again, he would have stayed away. We'll never know though, will we?" Momma asked me.

"I'm not so sure. Carson might not be able to tell us himself, but I'm willing to bet that Margaret can. Whether she will or not is another story altogether. It's going to be tough pressing her with Gabby standing around acting as her bodyguard."

"Is there any chance we can separate them?"

"I doubt it," I said. "Gabby can be overprotective when she wants to be. It's too bad we don't need to distract Margaret. Jenny confirmed this afternoon that she was working for her at For The Birds. Did you know about that? I mean before we followed Jenny back to her shop?"

"Of course I did," Momma said. "Phillip and I were in there last week buying a hummingbird feeder. The women get along remarkably well. It's as though they've been working together for years."

"I don't know. Sometimes you just click with someone else," I said as I rinsed the last plate and dried it. "I love working in the kitchen with you."

"I feel exactly the same way," Momma said. After she dried her hands, she carefully hung the dish towel on the rack, spreading it just so to maximize its drying potential. I did the same thing myself, a habit picked up from watching her do it a thousand times when I'd been a little girl.

"So, what else needs to be done here?" she asked me as she looked around the kitchen.

"That's it. We cleaned the front earlier, and Emma already took care of the deposit. I lost a little money today, but it's nothing compared to the PR nightmare I could be facing with the contest results today. I briefly considered cancelling both events tomorrow."

"You can't do that," Momma said strongly.

"I realize that, but it doesn't mean that I can't be tempted," I said. "Who knows? Maybe nothing bad will happen tomorrow."

"I'm sure of it, despite the rule of three," Momma said.

It was long believed in our family that bad things came in threes, but I was hoping that tomorrow would be the exception and not the rule.

"I'm ready to tackle Gabby and Margaret if you are," I told her.

"Lead on, Suzanne," she said, and we left Donut Hearts and headed next door.

It wasn't that far a walk, but every step felt heavy in my heart.

We were going to be opening some old wounds, and I already felt bad about doing it, but there was no helping it.

The truth had to come out.

CHAPTER 15

"I'M SORRY, BUT SHE'S CHANGED her mind," Gabby said after she answered our knock at the back door of ReNEWed. "Margaret doesn't want to talk to you. The past is just too painful for her to relive."

"She should be worrying more about the present, not the past," I said, speaking loudly into the crack of the open door so she could hear me. "We already know most of it, so she might as well talk to us."

"You're bluffing, Suzanne," Gabby said as she started to close the door.

"Am I?" I asked. "Ask her what happened thirty years ago. See if I'm bluffing then."

The door shut soundly in my face.

"I tried," I said as I turned to Momma. "I guess we're just going to have to do this without Margaret's cooperation."

"Hold on," Momma said as she pointed back to the shop. "She's opening the door again."

"Come in," Gabby said sternly. As I got closer, she whispered, "Suzanne, I'm warning you. Don't push her too hard. She's on the edge of a nervous breakdown as it is."

"We'll be as gentle as we can," I said.

Gabby had pulled four chairs together in the backroom of her shop, and Margaret was already sitting on one of them. Her eyes were red, and she looked as though she hadn't slept in days. "Are you okay, Margaret?" I asked her gently.

"No, and I'm not sure that I ever will be again," she said.

"You know that you don't have to speak with us if you don't want to," Momma said.

While I admired my mother's empathy, we really needed to hear Margaret's side of the story. "That's true, but it might just do you good talking to someone," I said.

"She's been talking to me," Gabby said fiercely.

"I mean someone who can be a little more objective about it all," I replied. "Gabby, everyone knows how big your heart is." It was tough to say without smirking a little, but the woman was fiercely loyal to those she cared about. It just so happened to be a very short list.

"How did you find out about what happened thirty years ago?" Margaret asked. "I thought that secret was long buried in the past."

"I spoke with a few friends on the condition that I wouldn't reveal their names," Momma said. "It must have been terribly difficult dealing with an unmarried pregnancy in those times."

"I was a foolish, foolish woman," Margaret said, her words coming out in a burst. "I was afraid that I was going to become an old spinster, and then Carson Winfield came along. He was young, and handsome back then, and he had an energy about him that was hard to resist. I hired him to do some chores around my place, and he did everything in his power to woo me. I thought we were in love, but when I found out I was pregnant and insisted that we get married, he told me that he was already engaged to someone else! He also warned me that if I breathed one word of my condition to anyone, and who had gotten me into that state, he would ruin my reputation forever. I was devastated, and back then it wasn't nearly as acceptable to keep a child out of wedlock as it seems to be these days. I went to a cousin's house in Atlanta, had the baby, gave it up for adoption, and then I came back to try to put my life back together. The reason I never married was that I couldn't bring myself to trust anyone after that." Margaret was telling us her tale through tears, and it was all I could do not to put my arms around her and console her. Momma was showing similar restraint. Even Gabby didn't stop her, which was to her credit, in my book. She merely reached over and took her friend's hand in hers, giving her what comfort she could.

"That must have been beyond belief to have to endure," I said gently. "Did Carson come to town recently to see you?"

"Yes, but not out of any love or affection. He wanted money. He desperately needed it, or so he claimed."

"What nerve," Momma said. "You refused him, I hope."

"I wish I'd been that strong," Margaret said. "But he warned me that if I refused him, he'd make sure that everyone in town knew what I'd done all those years ago. I couldn't live with the whispers and stares behind my back! I would rather kill myself than endure that at my age."

"So you agreed to pay him off," I said. "But then you changed your mind." I was leading her, hoping that I was wrong, but suspecting that blackmail had led to the man's murder, no matter how much he may have richly deserved it.

"Yes, but I had another plan ready, too. I knit, you know."

"We know," I said. "You filed the knitting needle down so it would break off inside of him, didn't you?"

"I got the idea from a tattered old paperback mystery novel from the fifties. Carson wanted every last dime I had to my name. I knew that if I paid him, I wouldn't be able to survive. Yes, I decided to kill him, but I didn't go through with it! You've got to believe me!"

"And yet he was stabbed in the heart with a doctored knitting needle," I said, trying to keep anything accusatory out of my voice.

"I lost my nerve at the last second," Margaret said, breaking down again. After a few moments, she collected herself and continued. "I threw the needle down onto the ground near the booth. When he asked me about the money, I told him I needed more time. He gave me twenty-four hours, and I ran away. Someone must have seen me wearing the scarf Gabby had given me. I went to her house and told her everything."

Gabby nodded. "Since Margaret didn't do anything wrong, I thought she'd be all right. I freely admit that I got too cute putting that scarf in the window, though. When you asked for it, Dot, I nearly had a heart attack, but what could I do? I *had* to sell it to you. Margaret didn't kill Carson Winfield, and that's the truth."

I wasn't sure if it was or not. After all, it made for an awfully convenient story. Her version of recent events *could* be true. Then again, she could just as easily have stabbed him, and realizing that we'd uncovered her motive, she'd come up with an alternate version of reality to try to sell us in an effort not to go to jail.

"What are you going to do, Suzanne?" Gabby asked. "Are you telling the police chief?"

"How can we not?" I asked. "He has a right to know what he's dealing with."

"But she just told you. She didn't do it!" Gabby insisted.

"Trust me, Margaret. You'll be better off if you tell the police chief everything you just told us," Momma said.

"But he'll arrest me," she protested.

"He'll question you, but I can't say if he'll arrest you or not," I chimed in.

"Give me at least until tomorrow," Margaret said. "Maybe he'll catch the killer without having to hear my story. You told me that might happen if I cooperated, Gabby. Please?"

"Pardon us for asking this, but what would keep you from running away?" Momma asked. "You've got to admit that you've proven to be a bit impulsive lately."

It was a tremendous understatement, but Momma had a point.

"I'll vouch for her," Gabby said.

"How can you stop her if she decides to flee?" Momma asked.

"She wouldn't do that to me." Gabby looked at Margaret and asked, "Would you?"

"No. I promise. If nothing has changed by tomorrow morning, we'll call the chief of police together. I swear it."

"What do you think, Momma?" I asked. I hated keeping this bombshell from the police chief for a minute longer than I had to, but then again, what could eighteen or twenty hours matter in the long run?

"I say we trust her," Momma said.

"Oh, thank you, Dot. I knew I could count on you," Margaret said effusively.

"Don't misunderstand me, Margaret. If you aren't here tomorrow at eight a.m., I will take it personally, and believe me, you don't want that."

Gabby looked as though she wanted to protest the overt threat from Momma, but ultimately she decided to stay silent. What was this power my mother had over people, and how could I acquire some of it for myself?

"Suzanne, is that agreeable to you?" Momma asked me.

"It will have to work, won't it?" I asked.

At that moment, Momma's cell phone rang, and after she glanced at the number displayed, she said, "I apologize, but I've got to take this. We will see you both here tomorrow morning."

"We'll be here," Margaret said humbly.

"I sincerely hope so." As Momma left to take her call outside where she could expect a modicum of privacy, I stayed behind for a moment.

"Gabby, thanks for coming to us with this," I said softly.

"If we hadn't, I'm sure that you two would have found out on your own. You already knew most of it. Suzanne, I swear, when you go after something, you have a single-minded intensity that I cannot comprehend. You're like a dog with a bone."

"Thanks, I think," I said, hiding the hint of a frown.

"It was a compliment, for what it's worth." Margaret blew her nose, and then her silent tears began again. Gabby looked at her friend with real pain in her expression. "I need to see to her. I trust you'll be as good as your word?"

"The way I see it, we have to trust each other at this point," I said.

"That's a fair point," Gabby said.

I walked outside and heard Momma wrapping up her phone call.

"Who was that?" I asked as she finished.

"My source," she said. "Suzanne, we need to find Arthur Bradshaw."

"Why? What did you find out about him?"

"Let's go. I'll tell you along the way," Momma said.

Once we were in my Jeep heading to Arthur's place, Momma said, "Apparently Carson was never good at making friends. Twenty-five years ago, Arthur threatened to kill him if he ever saw him again, so maybe he finally carried out his promise."

"What did Carson do to him?" I had a sudden thought. No matter how incongruous it seemed, the theory might just fit. "Was Arthur in love with Margaret himself?"

"No, but he was smitten with a local girl named Jillian Ashe. They were engaged, but Carson decided that he wanted Jillian for himself, and he worked his magic on her, just as he had Margaret."

"I saw the man. I've got to say, he wasn't particularly handsome," I said, wondering how he was able to weave his spells over so many women.

"From what I understand, he had a swagger, a confidence, that was almost irresistible to a great many women," Momma said. "You heard Margaret. Once she was under his spell, there wasn't anything she wouldn't do for him."

"I know, but I still don't understand it," I told her. "So, Carson broke up the engagement?"

"He did more than that," Momma said. "The young woman killed herself when she found out that Carson had just used her and that he was going to throw her away like yesterday's newspaper. In a fit of rage, Arthur threatened to kill him, so maybe he decided to follow up on his promise all these years later."

"Wow, it's hard to imagine committing murder after so many years," I said.

"Suzanne, look at it from his point of view. Arthur lost the love of his life, and we both know that he never married, just as Margaret didn't. I have no problem believing he could have struck when the opportunity presented itself."

"Then we need to talk to him and find out where he was this morning," I said.

"Shouldn't we tell Chief Grant instead of marching over to Arthur's office and confronting him?" Momma asked me. "It feels as though we might be taking an awful chance."

"Momma, it's what we have to do. This isn't without its risks, but what choice do we have? When Arthur was at the donut shop and word got out about me finding Carson's body, he was surprisingly quiet, especially given the fact that the man usually can't keep his mouth shut about the smallest thing. Remember, we didn't know the victim's identity at that point, so he had no reason to suspect that it was his old nemesis unless he had something to do with Carson's demise."

"What if Margaret wasn't the only one in town who knew that Carson was back?" Momma asked after a moment of thought.

"He could have been happy about the man's murder without actually committing it himself. Let's go speak with him. But I'm warning you, if he starts to get violent or aggressive, we need to leave immediately."

"Hey, I'm not willing to take any unnecessary risks any more than you are," I said, "but we can't let that stop us from tracking this killer down."

"Agreed."

Arthur was just leaving his office when we got there. Two more minutes, and we would have missed him altogether.

"Arthur, do you have a second?" I asked him as we approached.

"Not really," he said, clearly distracted. "My boss just called me. I need to meet with him in three hours, and it will take me just about that long to get there. What's up? You've got thirty seconds." To emphasize the point, he glanced at his wristwatch to confirm our time limit.

Okay, there was clearly not going to be an opportunity to ease into this. "We know about your relationship with Carson Winfield twenty-five years ago," I said.

Arthur looked at me coolly for a second before he spoke. "Yeah. I figured you'd be by once word got out who he really was. You're both wasting your time, though. I didn't kill him."

"You don't deny you had motive enough?" Momma asked him.

"Of course I did! He might as well have put those pills into Jillian's mouth himself. I loved her, and he took her away from me."

"You threatened to kill him back then," I reminded him, "and now the man's dead."

"It was a long time ago," Arthur said. "I hated the guy's guts, and if I'd known that he was back in town, I would have punched him in the nose, but I wouldn't have killed him. Am I sorry that he's dead? No way. That doesn't mean that I did it." He looked at my mother with disdain. "Frankly, I expect this behavior from Suzanne, but I thought ambushing someone in front of his office and accusing him of murder would be beneath you, Dot."

"We're not accusing anyone of *anything* at this point," I said. "Where were you at four o'clock yesterday morning?"

"I was in bed, alone. Where you were you?"

He'd said it sarcastically, but I answered truthfully. "I was finding your old enemy's body on the dunking-booth bench."

In response, Arthur just shook his head. There really was nothing else that he could say. "Sorry, but I can't help you with that."

"When you were at the donut shop and heard that a man had been killed, you didn't react at all," I reminded him. "Why not?"

"So what if I didn't? Is that suddenly a crime?"

"No, but it's certainly odd behavior for you. Why weren't you the least bit curious about it?"

"I've got other things on my mind, Suzanne. Something's been in the air at work for weeks, and I think I'm about to be fired. They're calling it downsizing, but the outcome is just the same. I'm too old and too specialized to get another job, and I've been hearing rumors for a while that this was coming. Now if you'll excuse me, I've got to go face an execution of my own."

After Arthur was gone, I turned to Momma. "Do you believe him?"

"It's truly a shame the way corporate America is discarding its most valuable and seasoned employees all to save the bottom line," Momma said.

"I'm not talking about him getting fired," I said. "Do you think he killed Carson Winfield?"

"I'm not sure. He might have, but there's no way of knowing, is there?"

"That's what we're supposed to be finding out," I said.

"Granted. So, what do we do next?" Momma asked me.

"I wish I knew," I said.

"We could always grab a bite at the Boxcar and see if Trish has heard anything," Momma said.

"Look at you, mining your sources like a real professional investigator," I said.

"Are you being sarcastic, Suzanne?"

"Not at all. That was sheer admiration on my part. Come on. Let's give it a try."

CHAPTER 16

"HEY, YOU! LADY! STOP RIGHT there!"

I looked up to see the stranger who had grilled me about Carson earlier, and he didn't look happy.

"May we help you with something?" Momma asked him curtly. She clearly didn't like the look of the man any more than I did.

"I'm not talking to you, sister," he said.

"Sir, I can assure you that you are no sibling of mine."

He looked at Momma to see if she was serious, and then he turned back to me. "It's just an expression. Why did you call the cops on me?"

"I don't know how much you know about small towns, but we here talk to each other. All of the time. I was concerned about the way you were acting, so I called a friend, one who happens to be the chief of police here. If you have a problem with that, then I'm afraid that's just too bad."

He wanted to be angry. I could see it in his eyes, but after a moment, his frown softened. "Yeah, I get that. I probably would have done the same thing. Anyway, I hear you're some kind of genius at finding killers. Is that true?"

"I don't know who you've been talking to, but I'd hardly call myself a genius," I said.

"Sir, what exactly is it that you want from my daughter?" Momma asked him, stepping in between us. Though she was much shorter than we both were, her presence was immense. She was protecting her baby, even if her baby happened to be a grown woman who was perfectly capable of taking care of herself.

"Take it easy, will you? I want to hire her, okay?" the man asked as he pulled a fistful of bills from his wallet. "I need to know who killed my friend."

There was a sudden softness in his voice and in his gaze that touched me. Perhaps I'd misjudged his gruffness and his outward manner and appearance. I put a hand on his and gently pushed it back in his direction. "Thanks for the offer, but I'm not for hire. I can promise you that I'm doing everything in my power to find out who killed Carson Winfield."

He looked at me oddly for a second before putting his money away. "If you aren't doing this for cash, then why exactly are you doing it?"

"You may have a difficult time believing this, but it's for the principle of the thing," I admitted. It probably sounded stupid to him, but it was what drove me in all of my investigations. "I feel that I have a personal stake in this. When I found his body, it became something I needed to follow up on, and when I learned that it was murder, it intensified my search for the man's killer."

"But you didn't even know him," he protested.

"I didn't have to. His death became a part of my life, if that makes any sense at all to you. I owe it to him."

"Okay, I get it, and I can respect it, too." He started to walk away, but then he stopped and looked at me a moment longer before speaking again. When he did, he reached into his wallet and pulled out a plain white business card. All it had on it was a telephone number. As he handed the card to me, he said, "If you ever need anything that I might be able to help you with, don't hesitate to give me a call. The way I see it, I owe you one."

"What kind of help could you possibly provide me?" I asked, curious about this turnabout in his attitude.

"Your only concern is to ask. It's my job to make it happen."

After he walked away, Momma studied me for a moment, and then she said, "Suzanne, you meet the oddest people in your investigations, don't you?"

"I seem to. At least it keeps it interesting," I admitted. "Now let's go see if Trish has anything new for us."

"Hey, ladies. Come by for a bite to eat?" Trish asked as we walked into the Boxcar Grill. It was well after five, and the tables were mostly full. "I'm sure I could squeeze you in if you give me a minute."

I knew Trish's methods of accomplishing that, and I didn't want her evicting any slow diners on our account. "Actually, we're coming back later to get food for our husbands," I said off the cuff.

Momma looked surprised for an instant, but she went along with it. "They've been working so hard, they deserve a treat."

"Trust me, they aren't going without. The two of them were in here not two hours ago for pie and ice cream," Trish said with a smile. "Those guys looked worn out. Whose idea was it to rewire and replumb the cottage?"

"Do we look insane enough to you to suggest something like that?" I asked her with a grin.

"I knew it! I'm not sure if you have a Plan B, but I'd start working on it if I were you. I give them until tonight, and then I'm willing to bet that they're going to call it quits."

"You don't say," Momma said with a hint of a smile.

"Dot, you're ready for the next step now, aren't you? You were planning on them giving up all along."

"I never said any such thing," my mother answered carefully.

"You don't have to. I can read it in your smile. So, if you aren't here for food, what brings you by? I'm guessing it's not just for the pleasure of my company, as pleasurable as that might be."

"We came to see if you'd noticed anything out of the ordinary since we chatted with you earlier, but we can come back later. You're clearly really busy right now."

"True enough," Trish said. "I have a few things to share with you, though." She glanced back at her patrons and added, "Don't worry about them. They can wait," she said as she stepped outside to the front steps.

"Are you sure?" I asked. "Don't lose any business on our account."

"Are you kidding? I'm practically the only game in town. I couldn't drive them away if I wanted to," she said. "Besides, this will only take a minute."

"Okay, shoot," I said. I knew there was no point in arguing with her. The only thing I'd accomplish would be to delay her return to work even longer.

"First off, there was a rough-looking stranger in here looking for the pair of you not half an hour ago. If I were you, I'd steer clear of him. He looks like trouble to me." Trish then went on to describe the man who'd just given me his business card, but I wasn't about to get into that with her. "Excellent. What else?"

"Margaret came by not fifteen minutes ago. She got a hamburger to go, and I'd swear it looked as though she'd been crying. Is she involved in this mess somehow?"

We'd given our word not to talk about Margaret's involvement in the case, at least not yet. "I couldn't say," I said.

"You couldn't, or you won't?" Trish asked me sharply.

"Does it matter? How did you leave things with her?"

"I was about to say something to her when Jenny came in. She saw the state Margaret was in, and she was quite unhappy with whoever got her all worked up. The two of them left together, and when I glanced outside, I saw Gabby meet them out front. Margaret took off with Gabby, and Jenny went off on her own. Folks are acting really strange around here lately, and it's got nothing to do with Fright Week. Or does it?"

"Was there anything else?" Momma asked her. Trish might have sassed me, but she wasn't about to give Momma any grief.

"No, I thought that was plenty," Trish said. "Did I help at all?"

"You very well may have," I said, not wanting to tell her that she hadn't shared any new information with us that we hadn't known. We were already aware of the fact that the stranger had been looking for us, and it made perfect sense that Gabby and Jenny were both looking out for Margaret. "Now get back inside and take care of your customers," I said as I gave her a hug. "We'll see you soon."

"I'm counting on it," she said. "Do me a favor. Once this mess is over, and I mean Fright Week and the murder investigation too, let's all sit down and have some pie and a nice long chat about it."

"You bet," I said.

Momma nodded in agreement. "Thank you for your contributions."

I swear it looked as though Trish was about to start blushing. "It was nothing."

"Perhaps, but we appreciate your aid nonetheless."

"So, we're no better off than we were before," I told Momma.

"That's not entirely true. It's nice to have confirmations of things we believe we already know. Shall we take a break from sleuthing and go see what our men are up to?"

"I thought you'd never ask," I told her.

We decided to leave the Jeep in the Boxcar Grill parking lot and walk through the park. It wasn't that we were trying to catch Jake and Phillip doing something this time. It was just a nice evening with darkness fast approaching, and I wanted to take advantage of it while I still could. Before we knew it, winter would be upon us, and my number of walks would drop with the temperature, but for now, it was cool and brisk, and a slight breeze made things even chillier.

In other words, the weather was exactly how I liked it.

"Hello, gentlemen," Momma said when we walked into the cottage together.

I'd been expecting more chaos than we'd witnessed before, but if they'd accomplished anything since we'd last seen them, I couldn't say what it might have been. "How's it going, guys?"

"I'll tell you one thing," Jake said, the plaster dust in his hair filling the air as he shook his head. "They sure make it look a lot easier on television."

It took all I had not to smile, let alone laugh out loud. It was a concession I wasn't sure I'd ever hear, and I didn't want to ruin it. "I don't doubt that one bit."

"Phillip, you look weary," Momma told her husband.

"Dot, if it weren't for Jake, I would have been home in bed hours ago," he admitted, and then he sighed heavily.

"I keep telling you that you don't have to stay on my account," Jake said good-naturedly.

"No, sir. If you're going to keep working, then so am I." After a moment, he asked softly, "How much longer do you think that might be?"

"Nine?" Jake asked tentatively.

"You don't have to prove anything to us by keeping at it," I told him. "We both already think you're excellent."

"As law enforcement officers, maybe," Jake said. "Remodelers, maybe not so much." My husband looked at my mother and asked, "Dot, is that offer to have your crew step in still open?"

"I'd be delighted to call them whenever you're ready," Momma told him. "There's no shame in admitting defeat."

Jake took his bandana, ran it across his forehead, and then threw it into the mess at his feet. "I'm waving the white flag and giving up."

"Your bandana is red," I told him with a slight smile.

"You get the point," Jake said.

"We were thinking about buying you two dinner," I said.

"Truth be told, I'm too tired to eat," Jake said.

Phillip chimed in, "I can't believe I'm saying this, but all I want is a shower and sixteen hours of solid sleep, and the shower is optional."

"That's what you think," Momma said with a grin. "Shower first, and then sleep. We'll be by to check on you both later."

"Don't rush on our account," Jake said. "Phillip? Thanks for your help. I couldn't have gotten this far without you. I'd shake your hand, but I'm too tired."

"Shall one of us drive you home?" Momma asked my husband in all seriousness.

"No, I should be able to make it that far, but I'm afraid you two are on your own tonight. Is that okay with you?"

"It's fine," I said, and I kissed him lightly. There was more than a little salty taste to it, but I didn't mind one bit. "We'll see you later."

"Thanks," Jake said. "To both of you."

"Why are you thanking us?" I asked.

"For not teasing us about this. We got in over our heads, and we both know it."

"We appreciate you trying," I said. "That's all that counts with us."

After they were on their way back to Momma and Phillip's cottage, my mother pulled out her cell phone and made a quick call. "This is Dot. Yes. It is time. Bring every able body to the cottage you can lay your hands on right now. Are you certain you want to work through the night? Very well. I appreciate that, and I know my daughter and her husband do as well. Yes, we'll leave the key under the mat."

"They're starting right now?" I asked her incredulously. It was late in the day even for folks who kept a normal schedule. For me, it was closing in on my bedtime before too much longer.

"They insisted. I believe everything will be accomplished before Halloween."

"I've never heard of a remodeling project taking that little time," I said. "Don't they need permits and things?"

"All of that has been taken care of. The mayor volunteered to expedite the process, and who was I to say no? He seemed to think he owed it to you as an apology."

"He didn't, but I'm glad to hear that we're okay," I said. "I'm not sure your workers are going to feel the same way about you."

"Ah, but these gentlemen wish to return to my good graces. They are delighted to get the opportunity. Mark my words."

"I've never made any money betting against you in the past, so I'm not about to start now," I told her. "The guys may not be hungry, but I am. Care to go grab a bite at the Boxcar?"

"Of course. I have to run an errand after we eat, though," she said as she patted her purse. "Do you remember the deal that fell through? Well, it's back on again. The seller seems eccentric and capricious, but I want what he is selling, so I'm willing to jump through a certain number of hoops to acquire it. Do you mind?"

"Not at all. I'll run all of the errands you'd like to," I said, "but only if you let me buy dinner."

"Suzanne, I take great pleasure out of paying. You know that."

"Sorry, but you're picking up the majority of the tab for the remodeling job. The least I can do, and I mean the very least, is pay for our dinner." I patted my jeans pocket and realized that I'd left my wallet somewhere, probably at the donut shop. "We need to stop by Donut Hearts first, though."

"We're not sampling donuts before we eat, are we?" Momma asked me.

"No, but I think I left my wallet there. Don't worry. It won't take a minute."

That was where I was wrong, though.

What happened next took considerably longer than a minute, and by the end of it, we'd both be lucky to make it through alive.

CHAPTER 17

"WHAT WAS THAT?" I ASKED Momma as we approached the front door of Donut Hearts. It was starting to really get dark now, and in a few days when Daylight Savings Time kicked in, we'd be in full night by now.

"I didn't hear anything," Momma said. "Suzanne, you really don't have to make such a production of things. If you want me to pay for dinner, just say so."

"Quiet," I said as I listened again intently. It was a dangerous move shushing my mother, but I had no choice.

And then I heard something again.

"Follow me," I said softly as I started walking around Donut Hearts to the back. Something was going on there, and I meant to find out what it was.

When I peeked around the corner, I saw Jenny Preston moving my trashcans around so she could spray-paint a warning on them. So far, she'd written, "STO," and I had a hunch what the last letter was going to be. It was in the same hand, even though it was printed in block letters, as the jack o'lantern writing I'd found earlier.

"Jenny, what on earth do you think you are doing?" I asked her pointedly as I stepped out of the shadows.

"Suzanne," she said loudly as the spray paint can dropped from her hands. "I can explain."

"You'll have every opportunity to do so in a minute," Momma

said as she pulled her cell phone from her purse. "I'm calling the police."

"Don't do that!" Jenny said loudly. "I didn't kill Carson Winfield!"

"I never said that you did," I said, watching her carefully. "Why would you assume that we thought that?"

Had Jenny killed the stranger after all? But why would she do that? What possible motive could she have?

Jenny glanced around, and then she put her hand in the baggy pocket of her jacket. "We need to go inside. Right now. Unlock the door, Suzanne." She glanced at my mother and added, "Don't call the police, Dot."

It appeared that we'd stumbled onto the killer after all, someone I'd barely suspected, and now we were about to pay for it.

CHAPTER 18

As I unlocked the back door of the donut shop, I said in the calmest voice I could muster, "Don't do anything rash, Jenny. I'm sure we can work this out."

"Are you, Suzanne? How can you be sure of anything? Things just keep getting worse and worse, and there's nothing I can do about any of it." She sounded as though she were ready to start crying.

The last thing I needed was a hysterical killer upset.

"Just put the gun away and we'll help you," I said.

"Gun? What gun?"

"The one in your pocket," Momma said.

"I don't have a gun. I was getting my lip balm out," Jenny said. "Why would you think that I had a gun?"

I took a deep breath, and then I let it out slowly. "Maybe we should all just calm down a bit and have ourselves a nice little chat."

Momma tried to subtly reach for her phone, but I shook my head. We didn't need Chief Grant, at least not yet. I wanted to hear Jenny's story and what had led her to this point.

"Like I said outside," Jenny explained, "I didn't kill Carson Winfield. I'm not saying that I wasn't planning to, but he was already dead when I got there!"

"Why would you want to kill him?" I asked her, clearly puzzled by the part she played in all of this.

"It's a long story," Jenny said with a sigh.

"My dear," Momma told her, "we've got nothing but time at the moment."

It turned out that she was wrong about that, but we didn't know it quite yet.

"I'm adopted," Jenny explained. "My folks were great, but when they died in a car wreck, I started wondering who my real mother was and why she gave me up. I dug into the old records at the courthouse and sifted through boxes and boxes of letters and documents my folks kept, all without any luck. I must have asked a thousand people a million different questions, all without any success. Then I got a break and found an older woman who was dying. She knew all about what happened, and she figured I had a right to know, so she told me all of it. That led me to April Springs after my divorce, and I opened For The Birds. You see, I was so obsessed with finding her that it ruined my marriage."

"Margaret is your mother, isn't she?" I asked as everything started to fall into place. I'd noticed how the two women had acted and looked similarly and remembered the bond they'd developed since Jenny had come to town.

"Yes," she admitted. "I haven't told a soul in the world that, but it's true."

"Does she know it?" Momma asked. It would have never even occurred to me to ask the question, but evidently it was a good one.

"No, and I can't bring myself to tell her," Jenny said, the tears creeping down her cheeks.

"So, you came here, opened your shop, and then befriended

her to get to know her. That's why you hired her, wasn't it? To keep her close to you?"

"I wanted to get to know her as a person first! I was about to tell her everything a few days ago when she confided in me what was happening with Carson Winfield. She was falling apart! It broke my heart not to tell her then, but I decided that I'd wait until this mess was all over and done. She told me she was meeting Carson at the clock, and I had a feeling that it wasn't going to be to pay him off. I couldn't let her do it! The only problem was that she must have gone to meet him early! By the time I got to the dunking tank, he was already dead! When I found his body, I was sure that she'd killed him! What could I do? I had to protect her. There was only one person I knew of who was normally out and about that time of morning, so I grabbed a mask and a broom and put it in front of the shop to warn you not to come out, Suzanne."

"It didn't work," I said. "If you knew me at all, you would have known that."

"I made a mistake," Jenny said. "Anyway, when I saw that he was already dead, I ran back home. I had to figure out how to protect her. The police didn't seem all that interested in Carson's death, so I knew that I only had to worry about you."

"You obviously left the warning pumpkin in front of my shop," I said. "Did you throw the trash-bag body into the road as well?"

"I figured it would take something dramatic to get you off Margaret's trail," she admitted. "I never wanted to hurt you. I just wanted to scare you away."

"The only thing you did was intensify my interest," I said.

"I can see that now, but my mother, my birth mother, can't go to jail. I'm only just now getting to know her. They can't take her away."

"She claims she didn't kill him, either," I said. I wasn't about to mention the fact that Carson Winfield, the murder victim, was her biological father. If she didn't know, I wasn't going to be the one to tell her. Let that secret wait for another day.

"But if she didn't kill him, who did?" Jenny asked.

"I have a sneaking suspicion that I know," I said. "I'm willing to bet that it was Arthur Bradshaw, and if we set the trap properly, I believe we can catch him red-handed."

"Very good, Suzanne. I knew that you were smarter than you looked. Then again, you'd have to be, wouldn't you?" Arthur asked as he stepped through the back door, a revolver in his hand. Evidently the door hadn't closed properly behind us, and he must have been standing just outside, listening to every word we spoke. "That pitiful excuse for a man deserved to die," he said as he came inside, "and I'm glad I got the opportunity to do it myself."

CHAPTER 19

"Y OU KILLED HIM BECAUSE OF your girlfriend all those years ago," I said. "Folks are going to understand your motivation. I'm sure if you turn yourself in, the jury will be sympathetic toward you."

"Maybe yes, maybe no, but there isn't going to be a trial," Arthur said.

"Why did you kill him on top of the dunking tank?" Momma asked him. It was as good a question as any, and I wanted to know the same thing myself.

"Carson was sitting there as though he was king of the world! When I confronted him, he was actually chuckling about something. The man had the nerve to reach out to me when he arrived! He said he wanted to make amends for what he'd done, and he hinted that he had a 'can't miss' opportunity he wanted to share with me as a way of making up for his indiscretion all those years ago, as he called it. Can you imagine that? He killed the love of my life twenty-five years ago, and now he was asking me for money! I agreed to meet him, even at that crazy hour. I would have done anything for a chance to pay him back for the heartbreak he'd caused me. I told him to come down off the bench, but he insisted that I climb the steps and join him. I had planned to make him suffer, but his arrogance inflamed me! I only wish I'd brought this revolver with me. I saw a sharp polished stick on the ground, picked it up, and then I pretended to hand him an envelope stuffed with newspaper clippings as I jabbed him in the chest. The thing broke off in my hand, and I panicked. I ran, and as I did, I saw Jenny coming around the corner of the hardware store right toward us. I climbed down and got away two seconds before she would have seen me, and I ran toward St. Theresa's to hide. I would have gotten away with it, too, if you hadn't started snooping around, Suzanne. You and your mother just couldn't let the police handle things, could you?"

"We did what we felt was right. Arthur, surely you can't kill *all* of us," I said.

"I beg to differ," he replied. "Don't get me wrong. I don't want to, but what choice do I have? I can't go to jail, not at my age."

"But Arthur, we're friends," I said. "Do you honestly think it's going to be easy killing me?" I was hoping to play on his sympathy long enough to come up with a plan. It was too bad the deep-frying oil was stone cold. There were a few potential weapons around the kitchen, but I had to be careful. It wasn't just my life at stake, but my mother's and Jenny's as well.

"You serve me donuts, Suzanne. That doesn't make us all that close. What's my middle name?"

"I have no idea," I said. "I'm friends with lots of people, and I don't know any of their middle names."

"Mine's Heather," Jenny said from one side of him.

"Okay, that's good to know," I said, wondering why she'd felt the need to chime in with such an inane detail. Then we made eye contact, and I saw her glance toward the back door. It was still slightly ajar. I'd have to get that fixed if we ever got out of this, but why was Jenny pointing it out to me? Was she hoping to run for help? I couldn't imagine figuring out how to distract Arthur long enough for her to escape, and even if she managed it, what good would it do Momma and me? Jenny might be gone, but we'd be left with a killer, and an angry one at that.

"Arthur, if you leave us here unharmed, I am willing to give you the cash to finance your escape," Momma said.

He laughed at the suggestion. "No offense, but how much could you have on you? A hundred dollars isn't going to do me much good, and I can't exactly take a personal check."

That was when I remembered Momma's errand. She was on her way to buy some land. I'd assumed it would be a banking transaction, but evidently the seller had wanted cash. She'd warned me that he was eccentric.

"Would twenty thousand dollars change your mind?" Momma asked as she started to reach into her purse.

"Stop right there," Arthur said firmly. "Don't move a muscle."

"I was merely getting the money to give you," Momma said.

"If you don't mind, I'll look for myself," Arthur said. "Hand me your purse nice and easy."

Momma shrugged, and as she started to hand him her heavy bag, Jenny made a choking noise beside him. When he turned to look in her direction, Momma struck him as hard as she could with her purse. It was as though the two of them had choreographed it earlier, but the results were not what they'd hoped for.

The purse glanced off Arthur's shoulder instead of striking him in the head. It did manage to hit the gun, though it didn't dislodge it.

I quickly did the only thing I could think to do.

I grabbed for the gun, and we wrestled for control as Momma recovered her balance and wound up for another swing at him.

This time her aim was truer, and it landed squarely on his forehead, knocking him backward against the outside door. His feet flew out from under him, and as they did, the gun went flying, landing in the vat of cold oil. Even if he could find a way to get to his feet again and recover the weapon, I doubted that it would still fire.

Jenny immediately sat on his chest, pinning him against the floor, while I grabbed a chair from the dining area and pressed it down on his neck.

"You can get up now, Jenny," I said as Momma took out her phone and began to dial.

"Did you really have that much cash in your purse, or were you bluffing?" she asked my mother as she stayed right where she was.

"I actually do have it, and I was going to turn it over to him when I thought to myself, 'What would Suzanne do?' Slamming his head with my handbag seemed to be a viable option, so I struck out at him. Sorry the first blow wasn't as effective as I'd hoped."

"You did great," I said. "The second one was a home run."

Jenny was still on top of the man.

"I can't breathe," Arthur protested as she pushed down even harder.

"Sorry about that," she replied, showing no real sympathy at all.

Ultimately it took two police officers to get Jenny off of him, and before she finally allowed herself to be lifted off, she managed to give him one last jab with the heel of her hand.

Margaret and Gabby were outside watching as they led Arthur away in handcuffs. "What happened? We saw the police cars from the window."

Jenny looked at me, and I nodded. "Now is as good a time as ever."

"You need to do this," Momma told her, and Jenny dipped her head slightly.

"Margaret, can we talk?" Jenny asked her softly.

"Of course, child. What is it?"

"I'm your daughter," Jenny said, and then she collapsed into the older woman's arms. The look on Gabby's face was priceless, and to my surprise, she was actually speechless, something that almost never happened with her.

"I knew it. Deep in my heart, I always knew it from the moment you came to town," Margaret said as she embraced her biological daughter. "Please don't hate me. I was young and I was weak, and I let my parents force me into giving you up. Can you ever find it in your heart to forgive me?" Margaret was crying more than Jenny at that point. I wanted to give them their privacy, but I couldn't bring myself to look away. It helped a little when I realized that Momma and Gabby were just as enthralled as I was.

"There's nothing to forgive," Jenny said. "I grew up with a good family who loved me. There was just something missing, you know?"

"I'd love to meet them and thank them personally," Margaret said.

"I'm afraid that's not possible. You see, they are both dead," she said.

When she saw Jenny start to cry again, Margaret held her close. "I can never replace them in your heart, nor would I want to even if I could, but I'd love to have you in my life, if you'll have me."

"That's why I came here in the first place," she said.

Momma touched my arm. "Suzanne, let's see about that meal you promised to buy me."

"I still don't have my wallet," I said as I saw two other police squad cars arrive out front.

"Then I'd be delighted to treat, especially after what just happened."

I agreed, but not before I stopped and gave my own mother a hug. "I love you, Momma."

"I know it, but not as much as I love you," she said with a smile.

CHAPTER 20

"I CAN'T BELIEVE THEY FINISHED THE cottage before Halloween," I said as Jake and I lay in bed, back home again in record time.

"When your mother sets her mind on something, she finds a way to make it happen," my husband said lazily. It was early for him to be in bed, but he was still feeling the effects of his labors.

"I appreciate you trying, though," I said, snuggling a little closer.

"As a handyman, it turns out that I'm an excellent law enforcement officer," he said with a chuckle.

"I think you're just about perfect, no matter what you do," I said with a yawn. "Can you believe that little Cindy Wilcox won the grand prize at the donut-decorating contest this morning?"

"Hey, her donut was the best one there by far. I don't even think the other winners minded losing out to a little girl," Jake answered. "I don't know about you, but I'm glad Fright Week is over."

"I'll second that," I said as I stifled a yawn. "Jake, there's something I've been meaning to talk to you about."

"Can it wait until tomorrow? I'm really beat," he replied.

I had to laugh. "Usually I'm the one conking out early. This will just take a second. Barton Gleason wants to lease Donut Hearts at night to run a little bistro there full time in my off hours. Our schedules won't overlap, and it might be a good extra source of income."

"Now that I'm not working, you mean?" Jake asked lightly.

"As far as I'm concerned, you *never* need to go back to work," I replied. "I'd be helping Barton out, and that would be nice. I know Emma would appreciate it."

"What do you think about sharing your space? After all, Donut Hearts is all yours."

"I share it with Emma and Sharon now," I reminded him.

"I know, but that's different."

"So, you don't think I should do it?" I asked him.

It was his turn to laugh. "Oh, no. I'm not walking into that bear trap. It's your decision."

"Aren't you even going to give me your opinion?" I asked.

"I'm sure you'll do the right thing, whatever that turns out to be," Jake said, and then he kissed me and rolled over. "Good night, Suzanne. I love you."

"I love you, too," I replied.

When it was time, I got up quietly so I wouldn't wake him, and as I took a shower, I marveled at our vastly improved water pressure. The workmen had done their jobs well, and I had to admit that it was nice having the place updated. It still felt like the same old cottage to me, which was all that I ever wanted. Arthur Bradshaw had been robbed of the opportunity to be with the love of his life, and Carson Winfield had paid the price for her suicide. Jenny and Margaret were getting to know each other on an entirely different level, and the town was slowly recovering from what had turned out to be a tumultuous week.

I myself was ready for things to get back to normal.

I'd consider Barton's offer, but for now, I wasn't going to do anything about it.

All I wanted to do was to live in my lovely cottage with my

husband, make donuts for the fine folks of April Springs, and spend quality time with my family and friends.

It might not have been enough for people who craved excitement and adventure, but for me, it was just about perfect.

RECIPES

Pumpkin Surprise Donuts

'Tis the season for pumpkin flavoring, and here's an old family favorite that I've tweaked over the years until we're all happy with it. The taste of pumpkin isn't overpowering, but it absolutely has the subtle flavoring we've all grown to love and count on in the season of pumpkins, ghosts, and goblins.

Ingredients

- 2 eggs, beaten
- 3/4 cup sugar
- 1 can pumpkin puree (16 oz.)
- 2 1/2 tablespoons canola oil
- 1/2 cup whole milk (2% will do as well)
- 1 teaspoon vanilla extract
- 4–5 cups bread flour
- 1 teaspoon salt
- 3 teaspoons baking powder
- 1/2 teaspoon baking soda
- 2 teaspoons nutmeg
- 2 teaspoons cinnamon
- 1 teaspoon ground ginger

Directions

In a large bowl, beat the eggs and then add the sugar, mixing thoroughly. Next, add the pumpkin, oil, milk, and vanilla extract, and then incorporate that as well. In another bowl, sift together 4 cups of the flour, the salt, baking powder, baking soda, nutmeg, cinnamon and ground ginger. Add this slowly to the liquid mix, stirring it in until it's combined. If you need more flour to make a stiffer dough, incorporate that now.

Chill the dough for an hour, and then roll it out on a floured surface until it's 1/3 to 1/4 inch thick. Cut out the rounds and reserve the holes to fry as well.

Heat enough canola oil to fry the donuts to 375 degrees F, and drop a few rounds into the hot oil, turning after 2 to 3 minutes. Remove them, drain them on a wire rack, and dust them with powdered sugar. For a twist at Halloween, follow Suzanne and Emma's lead and make the donut holes into eyeballs, using a round application of white confectioners icing, a smaller blue, brown, or green dot, and an even smaller black dot on top of that.

Makes approximately 1 dozen donuts and eyeballs.

The Lazy Person's Fried Apple Pies

These are great fun to make with kids, and we've been enjoying them for a very long time. When the donut maker (yours truly) is feeling lazy and doesn't want to go to much trouble, these are a wonderful alternative to some of the fussier recipes that are more standard for our household. Give them a try. I'm willing to wager that you'll find yourself turning to this lazy recipe again and again.

Ingredients

- Precooked apples with or without cinnamon, 1 can (8 oz.)
- 1 tablespoon granulated sugar
- 1 teaspoon cinnamon
- 1/2 teaspoon nutmeg
- 1 ready-made pie crust from the freezer section

Directions

Bring enough canola oil to fry these pies up to 375 degrees F.

Heat the apples in a pan on low heat, adding the sugar, cinnamon, and nutmeg, mixing well. Take them off the heat to cool. Unroll the pie crust, and flour the rim of a glass and cut circles out by pressing down and using a circular motion. A decent-sized glass will yield four pies out of one crust.

Place a small amount of the cooled apple mixture in the center of each dough circle, then wet the edges of the dough, fold it in half, and then pinch the ends together, sealing in the apple. The shape looks like a half moon.

Drop two of the pies into the oil at a time, flipping after three to four minutes on the first side. After eight to nine minutes, or until golden brown, remove them from the oil and set aside to cool. Dust them with powdered sugar, and they are ready to eat.

Makes 4 pies.

Gingerbread Bats and Balls

We like gingerbread year-round, not just at Christmas. It's amazing what a lovely flavor it brings to complement what can be an overload of pumpkin, from our coffee drinks to our tea to our donuts. We've modified the basic sticks-and-stones recipe over the years, and then we decided to Americanize it a little with a baseball reference. No matter where you live, though, these are really delightful.

These donuts are wonderful, a real gingerbread treat that fries up beautifully. I have to admit, I used to make these as regular donuts, but one day I decided to make logs and balls from the dough, and thus "sticks and stones"—now "bats and balls"—were born. They taste even better than the rounds, in my opinion.

Ingredients

- 1 egg, beaten
- 1/2 cup brown sugar, firmly packed
- 1/2 cup molasses
- 3 teaspoons ginger
- 2 teaspoons baking powder
- 1 teaspoon baking soda
- 1/2 teaspoon salt
- 1/2 cup sour cream
- 2 1/2 to 3 cups flour

Directions

Preheat enough canola oil to 375 degrees F to fry your donuts in.

In a large bowl, beat the egg, then add the brown sugar and mix thoroughly. Stir in the remaining ingredients, holding the flour until last. This next bit requires a bit of guesswork, so keep adding the flour slowly until you get a soft dough. Pull off four equal-sized pieces of dough about the size of your thumb and roll two into elongated sticks and two into tight balls.

Drop these into the hot oil and keep turning them until they are brown on all sides. Remove and drain on paper towels, and then eat plain, glazed, or dusted with powdered sugar.

Makes approximately 10 stones and 6 sticks.

Orange Drop Donuts

I love the flavor of orange in my donuts, so I make these when night begins to fall quickly and I need a burst of summer around the house. These donuts are light and fluffy, and as an alternative, you can use lemon, peppermint, or vanilla extract to give completely different flavors.

Ingredients

Dry
- 1 cup all-purpose unbleached flour
- 1 teaspoon baking powder
- 1/2 teaspoon nutmeg
- Enough canola oil to fry donuts

Wet
- 1 egg, beaten slightly
- 1/2 cup granulated white sugar
- 1/2 cup whole milk (2% can be substituted.)
- 1 tablespoon salted butter, melted
- 2 teaspoons orange extract
- Zest from one orange

Directions

Preheat the canola oil to 375 degrees F.

In a large bowl, sift the dry ingredients together, mixing the flour, baking powder, and nutmeg together.

In another bowl, combine the wet ingredients: the beaten egg, sugar, milk, melted butter, orange extract, and zest.

Slowly add the wet mix into the dry, stirring just until it is incorporated.

Drop tablespoon-sized balls into the oil, turning until they are golden brown.

Remove from the oil and drain on paper towels, then dust with confectioner's sugar or make a glaze using orange extract, a bit of zest, and confectioner's sugar, mixing until the glaze drizzles off the spoon.

Makes 5 to 9 drop donuts, depending on baking method.

If you enjoy Jessica Beck Mysteries and you would like to be notified when the next book is being released, please visit our website at jessicabeckmysteries.net for valuable information about Jessica's books, and sign up for her new-releases-only mail blast.

Your email address will not be shared, sold, bartered, traded, broadcast, or disclosed in any way. There will be no spam from us, just a friendly reminder when the latest book is being released, and of course, you can drop out at any time.

OTHER BOOKS BY JESSICA BECK

Baked Books
Cranberry Crimes
Boston Cream Bribes
Cherry Filled Charges
Scary Sweets

The Classic Diner Mysteries
A Chili Death
A Deadly Beef
A Killer Cake
A Baked Ham
A Bad Egg
A Real Pickle
A Burned Biscuit

The Ghost Cat Cozy Mysteries
Ghost Cat: Midnight Paws
Ghost Cat 2: Bid for Midnight

The Cast Iron Cooking Mysteries
Cast Iron Will
Cast Iron Conviction
Cast Iron Alibi
Cast Iron Motive
Cast Iron Suspicion

53952434R00104

Made in the USA
San Bernardino, CA
03 October 2017